SEVEN LIES

By the same author

FICTION

The Horned Man
The Siege and Other Stories (Selected Stories)
Three Evenings and Other Stories
The Silver Age

POETRY

Landscape with Chainsaw
The Revenant
A Jump Start
After Ovid: New Metamorphoses
(co-edited with Michael Hofmann)

SEVEN LIES

James Lasdun

JONATHAN CAPE
LONDON

Published by Jonathan Cape 2006

2 4 6 8 10 9 7 5 3 1

Copyright © James Lasdun 2006

James Lasdum has asserted his right under the Copyright, Designs
and Patents Act 1988 to be identified as the author of this work

First published in Great Britain in 2006 by
Jonathan Cape
Random House, 20 Vauxhall Bridge Road, London SW1V 2SA

Random House Australia (Pty) Limited
20 Alfred Street, Milsons Point, Sydney,
New South Wales 2061, Australia

Random House New Zealand Limited
18 Poland Road, Glenfield,
Auckland 10, New Zealand

Random House South Africa (Pty) Limited
Isle of Houghton, Corner Boundary Road & Carse O'Gowrie,
Houghton 2198, South Africa

The Random House Group Limited Reg. No. 954009
www.randomhouse.co.uk

A CIP catalogue record for this book is available from the British Library

ISBN 0-224-07592-6

Papers used by Random House are natural,
recyclable products made from wood grown in sustainable forests;
the manufacturing processes conform to the environmental
regulations of the country of origin

Typeset in Adobe Garamond by Palimpsest Book Production Limited
Polmont, Stirlingshire
Printed and bound in Great Britain by
Mackays of Chatham plc

Part of this novel has appeared in *Granta*

Every lie must beget seven more lies if
it is to resemble the truth and adopt truth's aura.

– MARTIN LUTHER

September 14

A woman threw her glass of wine at me. It happened at Gloria Danilov's party at the Temple of Dendur. I didn't know the woman – hadn't spoken to her or even noticed her. Gloria had just introduced me to Harold Gedney, who detached himself from me almost as soon as Gloria left us. A moment later this woman steps up: 'Excuse me, are you Stefan Vogel?' 'Yes,' I say, and without hesitation she flings her wine in my face. Red wine: a great spatter of it all over my chin and neck and white shirt. She walks away swiftly but calmly, no one stopping her, and from the stunned way people look at me I can tell the assumption is that I must have said or done something disgraceful.

I got out of the place as quickly as I could, not looking for my attacker, just wanting to remove myself from the situation, and walked all the way to the Port Authority.

'Excuse me, are you Stefan Vogel?' 'Yes.' *Splash!*

The sheer reflexive speed of it. The strange naturalness this gave the gesture, as if it were simply an inevitability, a law of physics, that the acknowledging of my name should trigger a little violent deluge of red wine.

I sat at the back of the bus, a pariah; marinading in the

clammy wetness. I was shaken, but almost more than that I was furious with myself for having come down to the party in the first place, against my own better judgement. And then, beyond both the shakenness and the anger, this *déjà vu* feeling I get in any crisis: that the attack only happened now in the most illusory sense; that in reality it happened a thousand years ago, and was therefore nothing new.

The lights were on when I got home. I took my stained shirt off in the car – didn't want Inge to see it – and put my jacket on over my bare chest, buttoning my coat up over that. Bundled the shirt behind a cupboard in the garage. Inge was downstairs with Lena, reading by the woodstove. She gave me her glazed smile.

'How was it?'

'Fine,' I tell her, 'lots of caviar.'

She keeps her eyes on me, trying – I sense – to resist the pull of her book. But if she has noticed I am home early, she doesn't mention it, and if she finds it odd that I am standing in the over-heated living room with my coat buttoned up to my Adam's apple, she doesn't, as I had predicted, want to get into a conversation about it.

After a moment she stretches and yawns:

'I think I'll go to bed.'

'OK.'

Another helpless smile, then off she goes up the little wooden staircase, Lena shuffling loyally along behind her, tail up like a bedraggled ostrich plume.

I came here into the spare room. Saw this jotting pad on the shelf – a spiral-bound notebook. The sight stalled me. I had a sudden, overwhelming desire to break my own rule of committing nothing to paper.

Some divination, maybe, that I no longer have anything

2

to lose? Some notion of what cataclysmic event must have occurred elsewhere in the cosmos in order for a woman to have thrown her wine in my face at a party in New York?

September 15

Walked up to the quarry. Purple starry flowers blooming over the ditches all the way up Vanderbeck Hollow. Maples and oaks still in their summer foliage, moving through the day like galleons in full sail. Though if you look closely the sails are getting tattered now, pocked and torn in places; nibbled by insects, the holes browning at their edges. Fall on its way.

Are you Stefan Vogel? Yes. *Splash!*

This desire to exorcise the past. Not only the remote or middle past (though that too), but last week, yesterday, just now . . .

RUSTLE OF newspaper from the study above me, the snip-snip of scissor blades: Inge working on her clippings. I picture her up there, pasting the heavy tidings of another week into one of the tombstone-sized albums she has been steadily collating over the years. As always, the image comes at me with the force of reproach; all the more painful for being unintended, or not consciously intended.

Snip-snip, snip-snip . . .

My undiminished love for her. Something in it verging on the idolatrous, as though for some higher creature that has come unaccountably into my possession. (Exactly how I feel about life itself, I realise: that it has come unaccountably into my possession, somewhat to its own dismay.)

3

September 17

A phrase of my parents' comes to mind, one that was forever on their lips or Uncle Heinrich's back in Berlin: *Nachteil kriegen*: to receive disadvantage.

Was that why I went down to Gloria's party, so as not to 'receive disadvantage'?

How in Berlin one was always in dread of not sufficiently abasing oneself towards some superior, and thereby 'receiving disadvantage'. Not that Gloria would have cared less or even noticed if I hadn't shown up. So perhaps more a sense of missing out on possible *ad*vantage? A reflex of my inveterate opportunism? Though what 'advantage' could have come my way at this late date, I cannot imagine.

Or perhaps I was looking for precisely what I found?

Are you Stefan Vogel? Yes. *Splash!*

Certainly I was apprehensive. Even debated whether to retreat as I came to the entrance of the party. I scanned the crowd milling among the Egyptian ruins. There were some familiar faces from our old New York days: the Chinese historian; that Czech couple we had dinner with fifteen years ago at their NYU apartment; the macho Cuban playwright who told Inge he'd written a part for her in his new play; one or two others – the remnant of Gloria's old retinue of dissident émigrés and exiles, sprinkled, as always, among her bankers and politicians. To the extent that any of them recognised me, they seemed friendly enough. Taking this to be an encouraging sign, I stepped into the fray, seizing a glass of champagne from one passing waiter and a black alp of caviar from another.

'Stefan!'

Gloria sees me from behind a pillar and sails over. Both

arms extended, her large old head tipped back in mock reproach, she takes my hands in hers, grasping them warmly.

'How kind of you to come! And where is your beautiful wife?'

'I'm afraid she couldn't make it.'

'Ah. What a shame. Give her my fondest regards. How lovely to see you! How long has it been? Must be five years at least!'

I nod vaguely, not wanting to discompose her with the fact that it has actually been more than ten since we fled New York and closer to fifteen since I picked up my last honorarium from the offices of the little Cold War quarterly she financed back in those days.

'Now you're living where, exactly?' Gloria asks.

'Aurelia. Up in the mountains.'

'I suppose you must love it.'

She looks at me with her kindly, guileless eyes. Her way of seeming only to acknowledge what is loftiest in one's nature, disregarding the rest, so that one feels gathered up for a moment, handed back to oneself in the form of a bouquet made exclusively of one's virtues and dreams and potentialities.

'Dear Stefan.' She gives my hand a little pat. 'Now, to whom shall I introduce you?'

The hostess must move on. But I don't think it's insincere, this warmth of hers. She must have kept literally dozens of us on the payroll of *The Open Mind*. Pure charity. A fervent anti-communist, but utterly democratic in her social instincts, as demonstrated by her choice of who – *whom* – to hand me off to:

'Hig!'

With a decisive movement she leads me towards a man

5

standing at the side of a cluster of elderly matrons. I recognise him immediately as Harold Gedney.

'Hig, I want you to meet Stefan Vogel. A wonderful dissident poet. He and his wife fled the former East Germany in – when was it, Stefan?'

''Eighty-six,' I tell her, bearing the various inaccuracies of her introduction in silence, as I must.

'Stefan very kindly read manuscripts for us at the magazine. Hig of course was on the advisory board. There, now.'

And with that, bestowing on each of us her elevating smile, she moves on.

Gedney turns from the ladies, sending a ripple of unease through their group. He looks at me with his pointed, ruddy face cocked appraisingly. I have been familiar with this face since my teens in the German Democratic Republic, where it formed one of a half dozen human images into which the abstraction 'America' would resolve itself in my mind. It was always gentle and frail and tired-looking, giving the impression of a sad god working overtime to help the human race, and now it is even gentler and frailer and more tired-looking than ever. The crest of sugar-white hair rising from his forehead looks almost ethereal in its silkenness; a veritable halo.

'A poet?' he asks – slight tremor of age in his voice.

I hasten to disavow the name:

'Well, no, not really. I'm –'

'I don't have much time for poetry.'

'Good God, I would hope not. A man in your position!'

Gedney gives me a circumspect look, as if unsure of my tone. I recall suddenly that he has been drawing fire recently, this distinguished elder statesman; a little late showering of opprobrium at the twilight of his career. I have heard his name mentioned in connection with the hostility towards

6

America currently surging across the globe. Even some talk among his enemies of bringing him to account for certain of his past actions and policies. I try to think of something I can say to show him I'm not being ironic; that I am on his side. But his hand is suddenly thrust out towards mine. I shake it confusedly, hear him say, 'Good meeting you, young man,' and stand there blinking as he walks firmly away.

Beside me the ladies dart reproachful glances in my direction. They must have been hoping to reclaim their high-ranking consort after he was done with me. Meanwhile, a young woman is approaching . . .

'Excuse me, are you Stefan Vogel?'

A fair-haired woman in a grey dress. Pearls at her ears and throat. Her face broad and smooth; rather pale. As she moves towards me I have the sense of a soothing presence coming into my field of attention. I do notice that she isn't smiling as she asks her question, but her very seriousness adds to her calming air. I look into her eyes, anticipating some balmlike, restorative conversation with her.

'Yes,' I reply.

And out of the points of light gleaming about her, the goblet of red wine, which I have not previously noticed, detaches itself, coming perplexingly towards me, in a perplexingly violent manner, its ruby hemisphere exploding from the glass into elongated fingers like those of some ghastly accusatory hand hurtling through the air at my body until with a great crimson splatter I am suddenly standing there soaking and reeking, blazoned in the livery of shame.

The shock, but then also that familiar, muffling *déjà vu* sensation; kicking in as soon as the shock wears off: the sense that despite the appearance of new damage, any harm done to me was in fact done aeons ago. *It has already happened.* Therefore nothing has changed. And therefore it is not important.

'I WAS BOUGHT . . .' Always imagined I would begin a memoir with those words if I should ever write one. A *me*-moir.

'I was bought' – instead of the usual 'I was born . . .'

I was bought

I was purchased

September 19

Tech and telecom stocks tumbling again. Good year on that front at least: accounting scandals, fear of terrorism, current administration's economic policy, all battering nicely at the markets. Even Intel's sinking. I shorted it at forty and again at thirty; now it's under twenty. Feels like betting on gravity, or on death.

This wondrous provision for gambling on failure! How it caught my imagination when it was first explained to me back in New York. I felt I'd stumbled on something like a professional calling. The first practical and profitable way I'd found of exploiting my own personality; my capacity for doubt, my tendency to expect the worst. I seem to have an instinct for companies in trouble; corporations with rotten wood under their gleaming skins. Too bad I lack the recklessness that ought to go with it. A little less caution and we'd be rich instead of just getting by. Own a nice house instead of renting this little cottage. Not have to rely on Inge's job at the health food store for our insurance. Would that have made a difference? I doubt it. Not that Inge doesn't appreciate the finer things in life (I always wished I'd been able to buy good clothes for her), but the lack of them is not what ails her.

Even so, I should like to set her up with a truly large sum, and for that, as for everything else at this point, my own annihilation seems increasingly the most elegant solution.

Convert myself into gold: one way of remaining with her for ever!

September 25

I walked Lena up to the quarry. She's still limping, but chased a squirrel and almost caught it too.

How Inge nursed her back to life after the truck hit her, instead of putting her to sleep as the vet recommended. Carrying her out into the sun every day on that wooden rack, till her pelvis healed enough for her to walk. Massaging her every morning, boiling hamburger meat for her. Then, since it seemed to help her sleep, bringing her up onto our bed at night.

My objection to that. Ostensibly on grounds of hygiene – her wheezing, her drooling and hair-shedding. But really it was just a kind of peevish jealousy that made me deliver my ultimatum: the dog or me.

I could swallow my pride and go back upstairs to our comfortable bed. There's nothing to stop me, and I believe Inge would welcome it. I could undress and climb in with her, find some way of opening a conversation. She would no doubt do her conscientious best to be responsive, as she would too if the talk should lead me to attempt more intimate things, though I know also the expression I would find in her white-lashed eyes (crow's-footed now at their corners but more beautiful to me than ever in their grave way, like two great aquamarines grown richer in their lights as their settings tarnish) if I were to lean over and kiss her: that papery look of good-natured effort and insuperable reluctance, flattened by each other into the same blank plane.

Fantastic freshness in the air up at the quarry. This autumn vigour that feels so like the energy of life, growth. Trees still a dusty, steely, end-of-summer green, but on a slope below me there was a single maple with half its leaf dome turned scarlet – *splash!* – like some trendsetter's bold new fashion statement; this year's embroidered shawl or silk pashmina.

I sat on a slab of bluestone in the rubble under the white birches. Burnt yellow plumes of goldenrod down by the old radio tower. Wild vines coiling all over its chain-link fence.

Inge, my Sleeping Beauty! Her spellbound air: deeper and deeper with every year that passes. Whose kiss will break the spell? Mine, if I can get this right . . . A farewell kiss.

Felt calm, looking out over the twilit valley, a bird singing its evening song from the cliff above me, birch trunks glowing like alabaster in the dusk. To disappear from this – like the swan in the poem stepping off from the solid ground of existence into the water; gliding there 'infinitely silent and aware'. Or would one just sink like a stone?

No concept of hell in the Bible. I read that in a magazine some evangelist group left in our mailbox. No basis for those lurid medieval fantasies of eternal torment. 'The wages of sin is death'; that's all. The unrepentant sinner merely passes into nonbeing: which after all is what he wants, increasingly, while he's alive; the prospect of new life being steadily more problematic and tiresome to him.

September 26

Another single tree turning – this one a delicate lemon yellow, a poplar down by the pond. Distant, intangible pathos. This other universe, with its own moods and meanings, its own not quite decipherable language for expressing them.

A word I learned recently: 'catabolic'. Having to do with the breaking down of organic matter. I see myself as a catabolist: my peculiar identification with this season, my gravitation towards autumnal things: forms, sensations, experiences, shaped by their relationship with the extinction towards which they are travelling, rather than the act of creation from which they sprang. The implosive beauty of collapse.

'I was purchased, my Uncle Heinrich informed me, for two truckloads of oranges . . .'

God! I can almost hear myself reading it aloud on one of those book programmes on NPR, though it would have to be some Hadean equivalent of that worthy institution, since the publication of such a document would of course be incompatible with my continued existence on this earth.

'We are delighted to have the late Mr Vogel on our show tonight. Mr Vogel, would you be so kind as to read us the opening passage of your memoir?'

'I'd be glad to: *I was purchased, so my Uncle Heinrich informed me, for two truckloads of Seville oranges. My wife, something of a celebrity in those days, was more expensive . . .*'

Do I dare?

To quote one of my own poems – ha! – Do I dare disturb the universe???

Do I?

But why this persistence in thinking I could possibly have

11

anything left to lose? Just the sheer habit of being alive? Haven't I always known I was going to have to break this habit some time? Well, that time has come! *Splash!* Inge, my darling, this is for you. I'd write it in German, but we fled that language, didn't we? Now I think in English, even dream in it. Here goes. Sell it to the highest bidder . . .

CHAPTER 1

I was purchased, so my Uncle Heinrich informed me, for two truckloads of grade B Seville oranges. Inge was more expensive. She was something of a *cause célèbre* in Berlin – a well-known actress in those days, as well as a prominent agitator in the peace movement – and the authorities in the former East Germany, whatever else they might have been, were astute merchants. For her release they demanded hard currency: five thousand dollars' worth of deutschmarks.

The money and oranges were given by the West German government to the Diaconical Work, a charitable trust of the Protestant Church, who in turn handed it over to the East German Agency of Commercial Co-ordination, *Koko*, where a friend of my Uncle Heinrich's was deputy director.

Such was the procedure in what was then known as *Freikauf*: the selling of dissident flesh for goods or hard currency.

On the eighth of June 1986, an overcast day with dots of moisture sparkling in the warm grey air, Inge and I were escorted in an unmarked van to the Potsdam side of the Glienicker Bridge, which we then crossed on foot, Inge's eyes full of tears, mine dry, each of us carrying two suitcases; without speaking, without pausing for breath and without looking back.

13

Two months later we were on a Lufthansa flight to JFK. The Muhlenberg Institute, an organisation of Lutheran pastors who had been in contact with Inge's father (himself a pastor, who had fallen from favour with the official 'Church in Socialism' for his work helping to reunite families divided by the Wall), had sponsored our immigration, guaranteeing a loan to help us settle, and lending us a small apartment above a homeless shelter in the East Village, which we were to supervise in lieu of paying rent.

We had had no intention of settling in West Germany, or for that matter anywhere else in Europe. America was always our destination. Nowhere else would do. In my case this was a straightforward decision: for as long as I could remember, America had been the point of convergence for all the unfulfilled cravings of my parched soul, and the idea of getting out of the East had always been inseparably bound up in my imagination with that of finding some way of transplanting myself into the magically enriching soil of the New World.

So far as one can ever account for such things, I suppose this fixation must have had its origins in my father's professional failure and the measures my mother then took to find other means of fulfilling her ambitions.

The chain of events began in 1974. My father, a lawyer by training, had been quietly consolidating a career in the diplomatic service of the German Democratic Republic, where his speciality was negotiating fine-print details in the Friendship Treaties springing up between the GDR and other countries in the Eastern Bloc. It was a humdrum if respectable occupation, but after the rest of the free world had followed West Germany in granting full diplomatic recognition to our republic in 1973, and the UN itself had opened its doors to us, my father was selected as a junior member on the GDR mission to that august body, and our lives looked set to change.

For a few months he shuttled back and forth between Berlin and New York: kindly, remote, befogged by jet lag and overwork, but always bearing gifts of a radiant strangeness – Slinkies, watches for deep-sea divers, a wireless that woke you with a cup of instant coffee. These little marvels formed the entire body and substance of my image of New York, and as I discovered many years later when Inge and I flew in, the picture they had created was strangely accurate: there below us were the toys and gadgets from that brief period in my family's life; metamorphosed into an entire city of hooped and flowing steel, of vast, luminous, multi-dialled watches, of buildings like giant radios with towers of glass and streaming water.

My father's visits grew steadily longer. There was talk of a permanent posting, even of our being sent out there to live with him . . .

New York! America! In those dark ages of absolute division between East and West, the very word 'America' seemed to bristle with dangerous, glittering energies. Like 'Moscow', it named the source of some ultimate fright and power. Bonn was our West German sibling: object of rivalry, contempt, occasional jealousy; but America and Russia were parental figures, and upon them we projected all our fantasies of supernatural and possibly cannibalistic strength. Nominally, of course, one was our friend, the other our enemy, but both gave us the same peculiar excitement to contemplate.

For my mother, the idea of our being sent to live in New York played directly into her sense of our family's innate superiority. She and her brother – my Uncle Heinrich – were of blue-blooded Silesian descent. Naturally this was not

15

something to brag about in communist East Germany, and they had been quick to drop the 'von' from the family name after the war. But in their quietly indomitable way, these two had maintained a sense of themselves as somehow ineffably superior to other people, and moreover they had managed to transmit this sense to those around them, not by any crude arrogance or self-aggrandisement, but by a certain aristocratic *froideur*; a mixture of haughty reserve and sudden graciousness, which bewildered people, intimidated them, and filled them with a kind of strained awe. My mother in particular was an expert in that particular form of psychological control which consists on the one hand in withholding, or at least delaying, a smile or word of kindness when the situation seems to call for one, and on the other in bestowing her approval of something – when she chose to do so – with a magisterial impersonality, as if she were merely the channel for an objective fact that had been handed down to her by some celestial source of judgement. The effect of the latter was to make one feel elevated, officially congratulated, as it were; as if a medal with the head of Lenin on it had been pinned to one's chest.

You might imagine that in a socialist society a personality such as hers, with the distinctly unegalitarian idea of life that it projected, couldn't possibly thrive. But somehow she managed to short-circuit the mental processes by which people might form a criticism of her in political terms, and confront them instead on a more intimate and primitive level of the psyche, where authority, if it succeeds in imposing itself as such, is unquestioningly believed in and – how shall I put it? – quaked before.

She was no beauty, with her sturdy little frame clad always in the drabbest brown and grey clothes, her crooked, slightly jagged-looking front teeth that dominated one's initial impression of her face, and made even her oldest acquaintances prefer to shake hands with her than exchange kisses. But there was something forceful, even magnetic in her appearance. Her dark brown, slightly protruberant eyes, encased in folded, lashless lids, possessed an unusual mobility and expressiveness. As they narrowed attentively, tilted to admit a faint sardonic lightness, gathered into their corners the traces of a codified smile, flashed with anger or coldly averted themselves from your gaze, drawing behind them an almost visible portcullis, one felt – with the fascination of seeing anything naked – that one was observing the fluctuating movements of the very organism to which the names Frieda, Frau Vogel, Mother, all referred. For as long as I can remember, there was a patch of pure white in her greyish brown hair, such as you see in certain city pigeons, and this too seemed the mark or brand of some quality that set her apart, though I was always uncertain whether it represented something done *to* her, or something she was liable to do unto others.

All of this – the haughtiness of her manner, the crooked teeth, the naked, imposing eyes, the little arctic patch on her head – was contained in, and to some extent tempered by, an overall burnish of tragedy; a kind of final, stabilising layer that had been added to her portrait during the middle part of the 1970s. This was the tragedy of thwarted ambition, and my father was to blame for it.

In his profession hard work and competence landed you in Hungary or, God help you, Romania; above-average skills might get you as far as one of the West European Permanent Representations; a certain type of well-connected career lackey would end up in Moscow. But in the private hierarchies of my mother's imagination, a mission into the *Imperium*

Americanum was an acknowledgement to those entrusted with it that they were the very *crème de la crème*, the crack troops, the elite. As our posting there grew more certain, all the chilly potency of that vast opponent seemed, by virtue of our association with it, to decant itself into our lives, and for several weeks we emitted an eerie glow among our friends, like that of immortals from legend, imprisoned for a term among mankind, but now at last able to reveal their true lineage.

Naturally my mother pretended to make light of these developments, even to disparage them. At the mention of America, or New York, or the United Nations, her lips would purse with a look of involuntary annoyance, as if some ancient personal grievance were being referred to, after which she would rather affectedly change the subject. Nevertheless, she saw to it that people were told of our imminent elevation. Allusions to my father's jet lag were dropped nonchalantly into conversations with our neighbours. Our friends in the Politburo, the Gretzes, were invited to dinner with Uncle Heinrich, who could be counted on to raise the subject with a twinkle of indiscretion, and thereby ensure that they were properly confounded. Heinrich himself, whom my father had helped get a job in the Office of the Chief of the People's Police, spread the word among our acquaintances in the security community.

Once, to my chagrin, my mother made an appearance at the school my brother and I attended, asking to be allowed to sit in on my history class. The subject was a comparative analysis of the emancipation of the serfs in Russia and the abolition of slavery in the United States. The idea being instilled in us was that the Americans had had no ideological interest in freeing the slaves, and only happened to do so by accident, whereas the Russians, as their subsequent history showed . . . et cetera. My mother sat at the back of the classroom with a stern expression. Halfway through the class she stood up and called to me in a quiet voice:

'Stefan, come with me, would you, please?'

Writhing inwardly, I rose and made my way towards her under the puzzled eyes of my teacher. We went to the office of the principal, whom my mother proceeded to harangue about the poor quality of the class.

'I don't see that the interests of our children are well served by quite such a crude portrayal of the Western powers,' she declared. 'I hardly think that those of us obliged to have direct contact with the capitalist system' – placing a hand on my arm – 'are likely to benefit from being taught about it in terms of caricature . . .'

I stood beside her; oppressed, heavy, numb; assuming the posture that now seems characteristic of my entire adolescence: hunched, eyes averted, blank-faced; a kind of permanent, petrified shrug.

The principal eyed us shrewdly from beneath her portraits of Marx and Engels. She must have been trying to decide whether my mother was raving mad, or was perhaps privy to some new educational policy development forming itself in the higher echelons of the party. Luckily for us she seemed to choose the latter. She promised to investigate the matter personally and see to it that the teacher in question was properly reprimanded. With a curt nod my mother thanked her and we departed.

The culminating act in her *folie de grandeur* (it amounted to that) came one evening while my father was away in New York. She, my brother Otto, myself and our 'lodger' Kitty (our maid in all but name) were seated at the dinner table, which, as usual, Kitty had covered with a cotton cloth before

19

laying, when my mother suddenly exclaimed, 'The linen! The von Riesen linen! We'll take it to New York!'

It turned out that a trunk full of family belongings had survived not only the war but also the upheavals following Yalta that had left my mother and her brother orphaned and penniless in what became East Germany. The trunk was in my mother's possession, stored in the basement of our apartment building. Among other things it contained a full set of Irish linen, including tablecloths and napkins, every piece embroidered with the von Riesen initials and family crest. Upon some fantastical new whim, my mother had taken it into her head that this linen, spread on a communist table in New York (I suppose in her imagination she saw herself as some sort of society hostess in the diplomatic world), would strike just the right note of mystery and coolly ironic humour, while at the same time impressing people tremendously.

'Nobody will know *what* to make of us,' she declared. 'And we won't explain. Just –' and she gave a sort of aloof shrug as if indicating to some fascinated inquirer that she personally had never troubled her head to wonder about anything so trifling as a set of initials that happened, yes, since you ask, to coincide with those of her own maiden name. On these rare occasions, when the outward guard of her demeanour was let down to reveal the rather childlike cravings and fantasies it served to advance, there was something endearing about her. Our hearts went out to her then; we felt we were being gathered into some rich and vulnerable conspiracy, and our loyalties were aroused.

Otto and I were sent down to fetch the linen as soon as dinner was over. To do this we had to get Herr Brandt, the janitor, to let us into the storage room.

'Try to keep Brandt from poking his nose into our things,

would you?' my mother asked. 'Not that we have anything to be ashamed of. But he can be a nuisance. Here, take him one of the miniatures and ask for the keys to let yourselves in. Tell him you'll give them back to him when you're finished.'

It went without saying that Brandt was a police informer, and my mother was probably right in imagining he would think it his duty to make a report on something even so trifling as the retrieval of a set of initialled linen from a trunk. It was also known that he could make himself obliging over practically any matter in return for small gifts, preferably alcoholic. He was especially partial to the Schaad-Neumann brand of aquavit, impossible to get hold of in the GDR, and my father made a point of bringing back a set of miniatures whenever he went to the States, for the express purpose of lubricating Herr Brandt. Thirty or forty of them were lined up in a double row at the back of a shelf in our larder.

Taking one of these frosted, cylindrical bottles, Otto and I went down to Herr Brandt's headquarters on the ground floor.

Ours was a modern building, constructed from the cheapest materials, but well maintained, and with a few grandiose trimmings, as befitted its inhabitants, who were mostly party officials of one kind or another. Four white pillars stood incongruously in the middle of the brick front, marking the entrance. The lobby was floored with polished slabs made of a pink and white agglomerate, like slices of vitrified mortadella. A bronze bust of Lenin, looking oddly piratical, stood on a plinth by the elevator, which generally worked. On every floor was a plastic indoor plant, the leaves of which Herr Brandt could be seen laboriously squirting and buffing on Sunday mornings. A powerful odour compounded of floor

21

polish and boiled meat pervaded the stairwell, and there was a more or less constant sound of toilets flushing.

Brandt was in the glass-walled office to the side of the main entrance, surveying the empty lobby with his usual dull stare. He wore a crumpled brown jacket over a sweat-soiled undershirt in which his womanly breasts and very large stomach bulged and sagged like pumpkins in a sack. Black stubble glinted on his whitish skin in the artificial light of the little booth, and the bulging roil of scar tissue between his throat and ear gleamed like satin. This scar, so he claimed, was from a grenade wound received during some battle on the Eastern Front. To my youthful and admittedly subjective eye, it was a decidedly unheroic-looking scar, and in fact had something furtive and guilty about it, like some malignant companion that had attached itself to this otherwise vague and uninteresting person. It was the scar – it seemed to me – that compiled reports on the comings and goings of the inhabitants of our building; the scar that had to be propitiated with bottles of Schaad-Neumann aquavit. Brandt himself gave the impression of living under its tyranny. For his own part he would have been content to pad around the place keeping the plants shiny, the floor waxed, supplying the tenants with cheap eggs from the poultry co-operative where he had a special concession. But some incomprehensible malignancy had settled upon him, and he was now its servant.

Once, when I was quite young, I had seen him carrying a parcel to the door of an elderly couple who lived on our floor. The parcel, which evidently contained either a mirror or a framed picture, slipped from his hands and fell to the floor with a smash and tinkle of breaking glass. He stooped down at once to examine it, prodding the wrapping with his fingers, an expression of grave concern on his face. Then all of a

22

sudden a most extraordinary cynical sneer took possession of his features. Fully aware of me looking at him, he dumped the parcel at the door of the elderly couple and padded off, shrugging as he passed me by, as if to say, *Nobody will know it was me who broke it, and even if they suspect, there's nothing they can do about it.* Furthermore, he seemed to convey that my having witnessed it, far from alarming him, in fact implicated me in the deed itself, making me no better than him. And the strange thing was, I did feel mysteriously implicated, and guilty too. It was the first time I had seen an adult do something patently and knowingly 'wrong', and the idea that such a thing could be came as a profound shock. From then on, whenever I ran into Brandt on my own, he would give me a contemptuous, almost taunting look, as though to say that he and I knew each other too well to have to pretend to be respectable citizens.

Otto told him we needed to get into the storeroom. He rose with a lugubrious sigh, evidently meaning to accompany us.

'No need for you to come,' Otto said suavely. 'Just give us the key and we'll let ourselves in. Here, this is for you. Compliments of the house.'

Brandt hesitated, holding the bottle in his hand as if he didn't know what to do with it. Then he winked unpleasantly – or rather it seemed that his scar winked – and unhooked the key from the ring at his belt.

The storeroom occupied a large area of the basement and consisted of a series of open cubicles behind a single steelmesh fence with a padlocked door in it. We opened this door with the key Brandt had given us, and by the dim light of a couple of naked bulbs found the cubicle that corresponded to our apartment, picking our way between the many glue traps Brandt had set out, in which insects and the occasional mouse lay in odd contorted positions, some of them still twitching with life.

There in our cubicle, among bits and pieces of old furniture which we no longer used, lay my mother's trunk: not so very large, but with ornate hasps of tarnished brass at every corner and great florid brass buckles that intimated a world of strange and remote ceremoniousness. I suppose I must have seen it before, but I had never taken much notice of it, and certainly never looked inside.

A sweet, mildewy smell rose as we opened the heavy lid. It was neatly packed, everything stowed in small boxes or bundles. The linen was in one corner, in a rust-coloured cotton sack, itself monogrammed with the intertwined initials and three falcons of the von Riesen crest. My brother looked on impassively, apparently less intrigued than I by this faintly mouldy-smelling exhumation of our family's past, while I poked around, turning up a set of silver spoons, an old marbled photograph album and a case of pocket-sized books beautifully bound in dark green leather.

'Come on,' Otto said, grabbing the pile of linen, 'the mother'll start fretting.'

I looked at the case of books. Of all things, it was a set of poetry: *World Poetry in Translation, Volumes I to VI*. I didn't know or for that matter care very much about literature, but I had an instinct for contraband, and the thought of anything – poetry included – that might not be officially approved of automatically excited my interest. I opened one of the books: poetry on one side, German prose translation on the other, but Otto was growing impatient.

'Let's split,' he said, 'it gives me the creeps down here.'

Closing the trunk, we went back upstairs, Otto waiting for

the elevator with the linen while I returned the key to Herr
Brandt.

Seeing me alone, the man immediately relaxed into that
familiar contemptuous expression.

'So did you find what you were looking for?' he asked.

I muttered that we did.

'And what was that?'

I looked at him, more surprised perhaps than I should have
been by this flagrant reneging on his tacit contract to turn a
blind eye: here after all was a man who had obviously broken
every bond of decency with his fellow human beings. His
face, or rather the swelling tissue at his neck, seemed to stare
at me with a brazen leer as if to say, *So what if I accepted a
bribe to mind my own business?* You *know me better than that*
. . . However, it was apparently out of personal amusement,
to remind me that we were both contemptible creatures, that
he asked, rather than any real interest, for when I said, 'Oh,
just a few odds and ends,' he merely gave a chuckle and let
the matter drop.

Upstairs, my mother and Kitty unpacked the linen. It had
lain so long in the trunk that the folds seemed to have made
permanent creases in the material, and the creases themselves
had discoloured slightly, forming a grid-like pattern over
everything we unfolded. But the silk-embroidered monograms
were intact on every corner, shiny as the calm areas on ruffled
water, and in spite of the poor state of the linen itself, my
mother still seemed entirely satisfied with her idea.

She and Kitty spent the next day washing the linen and
wringing it through the mangle. The following morning,
when my father returned from New York, he found them
ironing it in the kitchen.

It was evident that all was not well with him. Normally

25

he was fastidious about his appearance, careful to keep his wavy black hair well combed, aspiring to a well-groomed anonymity in his dark suits, plain ties and clean white shirts. Even after his all-night flights back from New York he would look spruce and tidy, if a little tired. But this time there was a strange raggedness about him: his tie loose, his shirt dishevelled, his jacket crumpled as if he had used it for a pillow. Most unusually, he had not shaved at the airport. And there was a haggard look in his red-rimmed eyes as they roved around the pieces of linen draped all over the kitchen.

'What's this?' he asked, turning up the corner of a table-cloth and examining the embroidered initials.

My mother told him, 'I thought it might come in useful when we go to New York.'

'Put it away. Get rid of it.'

It was extremely rare to hear him speak sharply to my mother. She retorted at once:

'What's the matter with you, Joseph? Didn't you sleep on the plane?'

'Kitty, leave us, would you?'

Kitty slipped out of the kitchen. My father waited till he heard her close the door of her room.

'Are you out of your mind?' he asked my mother.

'Joseph, please don't speak to me in that manner.'

'As if your family isn't enough of a liability already, you have to go flaunting your ridiculous heirlooms in front of strangers . . .' He waggled the embroidered corner at my mother. 'Von Riesen . . . What do you think this is, the Hapsburg Empire? The court of King Ludwig? Are you crazy?'

'I would hardly call Kitty a stranger.'

'You have no idea who she talks to.'

26

My mother's eyes gleamed dangerously. She asked in a tone of deadly self-control:

'Joseph, what is the matter? Did something happen in New York?'

'No!' he shouted. He seemed to quiver. And for a moment a look of fear crossed his tired, careworn face.

For my mother was right. Something *had* happened in New York. It appeared my father had made a blunder. What he had done, I learned later, was to have slightly overestimated his own licence to make concessions in the finer detail of an informal round of arms negotiation; a minute conciliatory gesture that he had believed himself empowered to offer, but which had been relayed to a member of the Soviet SALT II negotiating team stationed in Geneva and promptly aroused that personage's imperial ire. On the diplomatic stage at that particular moment in history, when the two sides of the globe had worked themselves into an inflammable sweat of paranoid terror about each other's intentions, the smallest things were charged with an exaggerated significance. There was the well-known incident of the Soviet official who forgot to remove his hat when he greeted President Nixon in Moscow for the signing of the SALT I treaty. The negligence was interpreted by the Americans as a deliberate affront, and the newspapers spent many days speculating on what precise grievance was being symbolically expressed. Given that this year, the year of my father's blunder, happened to be the very year in which our state was prevailed upon to change its constitution, and proclaim itself 'for ever and irrevocably allied' with the Soviet Union, my father had good reason to be worried. History doesn't relate what happened to the official who forgot to take off his hat, but there is little reason to believe that he was forgiven for his error.

At any rate, my father wasn't. A few days after his return he was told that he had been removed from the UN team.

My father must have guessed that that was to be his last trip; in addition to the usual case of miniatures for bribing Herr Brandt, he had brought with him presents of an especially poignant 'Americanness': a raccoon-skin hat for my mother, a New Mexican turquoise pin for Kitty, a calculator for Otto, and for me a set of metal ballpoint pens, each in the shape of a famous American skyscraper. These joined the other knick-knacks and gadgets he had brought home on earlier trips, and because they were now part of a finite series, never to be further augmented, they acquired a hallowed quality in our household. They were the sacred relics of a brief, visionary connection with a reality larger than our own; one that had tragically eluded our grasp.

CHAPTER 2

So much for my family's glorious ascent into the international political elite of New York.

To my mother's credit, she never directly reproached my father, but the tragic aura she assumed from then on must have been a living reproach to him, and even if it wasn't, he certainly subjected himself to enough reproach of his own. Quite a rapid change came over him: he continued to work hard (he was sent back to the Friendship Treaties, and the subsequent agreements on technology-sharing with other Warsaw Pact countries), but under what seemed a steadily thickening glaze of failure. He wasn't the type to respond to criticism from his superiors with defiance or countercriticism. What he seemed to want were opportunities to show his loyalty and diligence, if not in order to be reinstated, then at least to be acknowledged as a faithful servant. At the same time, though, he had obviously lost his self-confidence, and with it the air of quiet capability that had once impressed people, so that even if his blunder had been forgiven, he was clearly no longer suitable for a high-level career in the diplomatic service. His appearance grew shabbier. He aged. There was something distracted and disconcertingly meek in the way he smiled.

As for my mother's 'tragic aura', it was a complex thing; a

hybrid, I believe, of real disappointment, and a kind of tactical reorganisation of her forces. There was humility in it – just enough to deflect the *Schadenfreude* or downright vengeful delight of her acquaintances, and to convert what had formerly been a rather too flagrant haughtiness into something more subtle and sombre and dignified. If she could no longer intimidate people by the suggestion of hidden powers in her possession, she could make them respect her out of consideration for the magnitude of our loss. She made a point of telling our friends and neighbours what had happened, always in a tone of sad but unselfpitying acceptance of our misfortune, thereby establishing the event in terms that were acceptable to her, and gaining control over people's reactions to it.

It was at this time that the word 'intellectual' first entered her active vocabulary. Pretty soon it was joined by other, similar words, such as 'cultural' and 'aesthetic'. 'So and so is an *intellectual* fraud,' she might be heard saying, or 'So and so has no *aesthetic* sense whatsoever.'

At first these remarks had a tentative quality, like somebody trying out a new way of dressing and pretending not to be anxious about what others might think. But people seemed to accept them without protest, and the self-consciousness soon left her. Before long it was apparent that she had constructed a new hierarchy of values by which to organise the world in a manner that once again accorded with her invincible sense of our family's worth. If we were not to take our place in the inner circle of the political elite, then so be it: we would dazzle and confound others from our eminence in the sphere of *real merit*, which was to say the sphere of culture and ideas and, above all, *Art*.

Given that none of us had accomplished anything at all in this sphere, her successful transformation of our whole tone and image as a family must be counted as quite a triumph. Her own education had been a ramshackle affair, interrupted by the war (though she claimed to have had a tutor at the age of eleven who had made her read 'everything'), but her brother Heinrich had been through university, and at one time contemplated a career as a man of letters. He still subscribed to the official literary publications, and in his position as senior counsel at the Office of the Chief of the People's Police, he had easy access to the best artistic circles, which from time to time he still frequented. Naturally my mother enlisted him in her new project. And doting on her as he did (he had no family of his own), he was happy to oblige.

A new phase of our life began. Uncle Heinrich introduced my mother to a number of officially recognised writers and artists of his acquaintance. We dutifully made the round of their plays, concerts and exhibitions, mingling with them afterwards, and before long they began appearing at our apartment on Micklenstrasse. Naturally obsequious as a breed, and knowing of my mother only that she was the sister of an important government functionary who took an interest in the arts, they were never difficult to entice. In a remarkably short space of time, through sheer force of will, as well as that curious hypnotic power of suggestion that gathered people like sheep into her private fantasies, she turned our household into a gravitational centre for artists and intellectuals of every stripe. My father acquiesced in his meek way. Once, timidly, he asked if she was sure she wasn't going to 'receive disadvantage' for associating with the wrong types, but he was quickly silenced by her acid retort that she hardly thought her brother would be introducing her to charlatans of the kind he was obviously referring to.

The apartment itself underwent a transformation. Framed

prints and reproductions went up. In time, as my mother's patronage grew, artists began presenting her with original oils and watercolours, and these joined the reproductions on the walls. There were even some sculptures which, like the paintings, were both representational and at the same time sufficiently unrealistic in their distortions and bulbous excrescences to indicate that their creators were fully abreast of the latest developments in modern art. Furthermore, they were uniformly of what I would call an 'aspiring' tone. Eyes and hands were often raised upwards in a slyly sublime manner. The darker, more turbulent works were sure to have gleams of light peeping over some horizon in the background.

The most 'aspiring' of them all was a life-sized bronze statue representing a naked female dancer reaching towards the heavens. Her arms and hands were immensely thin and elongated, as if the intensity of her 'aspiration' had literally stretched her about five inches. Her thin legs were more like a flamingo's than a human's. Interestingly, though, as if distracted from his lofty purpose by a momentary lasciviousness, the artist had endowed her with full, upward-curving, gravity-defying breasts, which he had very carefully modelled to show the nipples and areolas in minute detail. Otto in particular was fascinated by these breasts, and when our parents were not about, he would entertain me by slinking up behind the girl and grabbing hold of them, murmuring delirious blandishments into her bronze ear. Kitty was embarrassed by her, and could be made to blush when circumstances forced her to acknowledge her presence. My father also objected to her, ostensibly on the grounds that she occupied more than her fair share of the living room. But my mother had pronounced this figure an 'aesthetic triumph', and we were given notice that anyone who criticised her ran

32

the risk of being stigmatised as 'visually blind' – one of her most deadly put-downs at this time.

It was during this period that I first heard myself being referred to as the family 'poet-intellectual'. It was done so casually that I didn't consciously notice it until it had insinuated its way into my own image of myself. I therefore didn't react to it with the suspicion or perplexity I should have. As our artistic gatherings consolidated themselves into regular soirées and I heard my mother introduce me as our 'literary man', our own 'poet-intellectual', often adding, 'He reads *all* the time. It's impossible to drag him away from a book once he's started; just like I was at his age,' I felt it as one of those immemorial truths about oneself that are so well established they are almost too boring to mention. It was as if she had said, *He's rather small for his age*, or *He's always had a sweet tooth*. The fact that I had never written a poem, and that I never read a book unless I had to for class, was neither here nor there. The idea was like one of those cloud-forest plants that subsist on air and light alone. It appeared to require no nourishment from reality in order to grow, either in my own mind or in the minds of our acquaintances. Before long it became absorbed into the conversational ritual at our monthly soirées, where guests suffering from the slight awkwardness entailed in talking to the adolescent children of their hostess could now inquire after my poetry. 'How's the writing going?' they might say with a look of respectful concern – or, more facetiously, with a little motion of their wrists, 'Still scribbling away?' – to which I would respond with a vague nod and what I hoped was a tantalisingly elusive smile, before changing the subject.

There was an upright piano in the corner of the living room, and from time to time there would be music at our gatherings: a solo recital by some budding young pianist, or a trio or quartet if others brought instruments. Given the obdurately stiff, formal, frosty tenor of the conversational part of the soirées, these interludes were a relief to the company and always greatly appreciated. One day a lull descended on the room when there happened to be no musicians present. A writer named Franz Erhardt stepped forward and 'begged permission' to read us something from his novel, which he had brought with him. Permission was granted, and he began to read.

He was a small, sallow man with a forked beard and light blue eyes that always seemed to be at work on some caustic or double-edged little observation. My mother had found him a job at the state TV company, and he told me once, with a strange sort of rueful sneer, that he occasionally dreamed of her, 'just as the English dream of their queen'. I understand that he went on to become quite a success in the literary world of the GDR, and that by the time the Wall came down he was a top-ranking bureaucrat in the Writers' Union, with guaranteed sales of a hundred thousand copies of every novel he wrote. A few years ago I read in the *New York Times* that he had hanged himself after his Stasi file had been opened, revealing that he had been an informer for most of his adult life. I remember that the novel he read from that evening was a strange sort of satirical spoof, unusual in those days of solid socialist realism, taking as its premise President Kennedy's famous statement '*Ich bin ein Berliner*' and imagining a patrician American with Kennedy's decadent appetites and corrupt ideas getting stuck in East Berlin and suffering a series of instructive mishaps that finally turn him into a good and happy socialist.

Judging from the hearty laughter that filled the room, it

had plenty of funny jokes. I myself was too young to understand them. Besides, I was distracted. There was something
about the very fact of this reading – a novelty in our drawing
room – that was making me uneasy. I noticed my Uncle
Heinrich staring at me pensively once or twice across the
room. For some time I had been dimly aware of his interest
in me growing more intense, as if my 'writing' and his own
former literary ambitions made us kindred spirits. He would
often talk to me about writers he admired, sometimes
discussing his own youthful efforts, and telling me how much
he looked forward to reading something of mine. For my part
the whole subject occupied such a dreamy, subterranean part
of my consciousness that I find it almost hard to accuse myself
of active hypocrisy in allowing him to continue in his delu-
sions about me.

But as I watched him now, his cropped head with its
elegant, gaunt features and silver-grey eyes roving attentively
between Erhardt, the enrapt guests and myself, I had a faintly
sickening sensation that some hidden and intimate area of
myself that I had until now considered inviolably private was
about to be forcibly exposed to public view.

Sure enough, as soon as the reading was over and the
applause had begun to die down, I heard my uncle's rather
high-pitched voice with its clipped enunciation, calling to me
from across the room.

'Stefan, young fellow, what about you? Why don't you read
something of yours now?' He was looking at me with a kindly
expression – there was always something very proper and clean
and good-natured about him; *merry*, one might almost say –
but at that moment his smiling face seemed to me full of
menace and barely concealed cruelty. I remember observing
the same dignified and innocent expression of warmth on his

face and feeling the same chilled response in my own heart many years later, when I was brought to him in his comfortable rooms at the Office of the Chief of the People's Police, where once again I found myself at a loss to circumvent some request that from his point of view was wholly reasonable, while to me it seemed to stretch the already abused fabric of my soul to the point of ripping it altogether in two.

His suggestion was immediately taken up by the other guests.

'Yes, what a good idea,' a voice cried out. 'Frau Vogel, ask your son to read us one of his compositions.'

'I – I don't have anything prepared,' I stammered. But my apparent modesty merely fanned the flames of their interest, and I soon found myself at the centre of a chorus of bantering remarks about my shyness and lack of spontaneity. 'Come on, Stefan, read us something from this great work we've been hearing so much about,' someone called, while another, to my mortification, said, 'Otto, fetch your brother's poems. He's too modest to get them himself.'

Otto turned to this speaker with the look of surly impassiveness that he had been perfecting over the past year. He too had been a target for my mother's 'artistic' reinvention of our family. Since he had always been good with his hands, he was chosen to represent the pictorial muse. He had been sent to drawing classes and presented with a box of high-grade French charcoals and some handmade paper sketchbooks finagled by my mother through our surviving connections in the higher levels of the *privilegentsia*. After the first few classes he had abruptly refused to attend any more. My mother tried to change his mind, but he stood his ground. Even when she rather unsubtly attempted to pander to his burgeoning interest in girls by offering to find him a class

36

with live nude models, he resisted. And when finally she threatened to punish him if he didn't keep at it, he broke the charcoals, ripped the sketchbooks to pieces and exploded at her with such savage virulence that she – even she – had been forced to back down. Otto now occupied an anomalous, private, decultured zone within the family: tolerated, but not much more.

I'm not sure whether I simply lacked his courage to be himself, or whether I had allowed myself to become tainted by the thought that I might actually be that potent and glamorous thing, an artist. Perhaps, despite my shyness and horror of exposure, I secretly craved the kind of attention that had just been lavished on Franz Erhardt. Instead of coming out and confessing that I didn't in fact have anything to read to the assembled company, I merely stood there, inwardly writhing, unable to speak, while the guests continued baying at me from all corners of the room.

It was my father, to my surprise, who saved me, though it would certainly have been better for me in the long run if he hadn't.

'Perhaps next time, Stefan, eh?' he said quietly. 'That way you'll have time to prepare something for us.'

It was so rare for him to assert himself in any way at these gatherings that I think people in their uncertainty attributed more authority to him than he actually possessed. He was deferred to: the baying stopped, and with a few waggings of fingers and stern warnings not to forget, I was given a month's reprieve.

As THE DAYS passed, the question of how I was going to acquit myself at the next soirée grew rapidly from a faint unease to a consuming preoccupation that soon formed the single focus of my life. Theoretically it still would have been possible to own up to my lack of material and back down, but as I have often felt when faced with a choice between a healthy and a harmful course of action, I had the distinct sensation of the harm *having already been done*, without my conscious consent or even participation, so that the apparent choice was in fact no choice at all. At any rate, the thought of making a clean breast of things, disgracing myself before my mother and looking foolish in front of her friends barely crossed my mind. With the same odd mixture of submissiveness and furtive ambition, I lay awake at nights, next to my sleeping brother, racking my brains for a solution. I had tried the most rational thing: to sit down and write. But it had become painfully clear to me that whatever faculties of imagination and verbal ingenuity were required to bring something even remotely coherent, let alone interesting, into existence on a blank page, I was entirely devoid of them. The feeling I'd had as I sat at my table trying to coax words out of myself was more than simply one of impotence; it was a kind of vast, inverted potency: the sheer inert mass of blankness that I had attempted to breach reverberating violently back through me, as though I had tried to smash through a steel door with my fist. I soon gave up.

It was on a morning a few days before the soirée that my anxiety, roused by now to a condition in which it actually functioned as a kind of substitute imagination, formed the first in what turned out to be a long series of dubious solutions, each of which immediately raised new and more serious problems.

As Kitty opened the larder in search of some jam for my mother's toast, I happened to glimpse the double row of aquavit bottles at the back of the top shelf. Unreplenishable since my father's fall from grace, these had now acquired the value of precious heirlooms, and my parents were extremely sparing in their use of them as bribes. From the sight of these bottles, my mind turned to Herr Brandt, and from him to the last expedition Otto and I had made to the basement, in search of the von Riesen linen. And suddenly I remembered those leather-bound volumes of *World Poetry in Translation*.

That afternoon, during the quiet hour after my return from school, when my parents were both out and Kitty was in her room enjoying a moment of leisure before preparing our dinner, I stole one of the little frosted-glass bottles from the larder and went downstairs to ask Brandt for the key to the storage room. He stared at me, so long, and with such vacant dullness, that for a moment I wondered if he now considered it so far beneath his dignity to acknowledge me that I had actually become invisible to him. But eventually he gave his weary sigh and got up to accompany me.

Doing my best to imitate my brother's confident, worldly tone, I told him I could manage on my own, if he would just give me the key. I took out the aquavit bottle and nonchalantly offered it to him. 'Here, this is for you. Compliments of the house.' A glint of something approaching amusement appeared in his eye. My contemptible absurdity had apparently just sunk to new depths of preposterousness. He took the bottle with a disdainful shrug of his heavy, soft shoulders. I waited for him to give me the key, but he merely looked at the bottle, wiping the mist from the frosted glass with the pad of a thumb so fleshy and nail-bitten it looked like one of those pastries where the risen dough all but engulfs the dab of jelly at its centre.

'Could I have the key, please?' I asked, attempting to control

39

a faint tremor in my voice. Herr Brandt smiled and raised two obese fingers. '*Zwei Flaschen*,' he said, 'one for privacy, one for the key.' It struck me that the peculiar warped affinity that existed between us had somehow made it apparent to him that I was here on personal rather than family business, and with his lugubrious but unerring instinct for such things, he realised he had found an opportunity for extortion. Aware of my own powerlessness as well as the jeopardy I had placed myself in, I swallowed my protests and went silently back upstairs for a second bottle.

Kitty was now in the kitchen peeling potatoes. It was imperative that I get her out immediately: I sensed that if I were gone longer than a minute or two Brandt would consider himself justified in renegotiating the terms. I could picture exactly the ponderous way he would look at his watch and shrug off any attempt to hold him to his word. As is often the case with me, acute necessity brought forth invention – or at least a short-term expedient. I remembered that Kitty had been unhappy a few weeks ago when some man she had been seeing had suddenly vanished. Tearfully she had admitted to my mother that the man had been a member of a group that met once a week in a church to discuss world peace. Thinking he had been arrested, she had begged my mother to use her influence to help him. My mother had retorted with a stern lecture on the impropriety of a member of our household having anything to do with such a person, and that was the last I had heard of the matter.

'Jürgen's outside,' I told Kitty. 'He asked me to come and get you. He's in the alley by the coal-hole. He looks like he's been living rough.'

Gasping, Kitty ran out of the room, her hands still wet from the potatoes. I took the second bottle, rearranging some

40

canned celery to fill the space at the end of the row, and, with a feeling of venom in my heart, went back downstairs.

This time I was careful not to give Brandt the bottle until I had the key. Even so, he managed to make me jump through one more hoop. Instead of actually handing me the key, he merely pointed to the bunch hanging at his waist and told me to come and unhook it myself. This I did, reluctantly, but feeling that I had no choice. As I fumbled with the key ring, I was unpleasantly aware of his sour smell and the soft paunch of his stomach wobbling against the back of my wrist.

With the key finally in my hand, I went down to the basement. Only one of the two bulbs hanging in the storeroom worked, and the place was gloomier than ever. The trunk's brasswork gleamed faintly among the shadowy bric-a-brac of our cubicle. I opened the lid, releasing the familiar musty odour, and took out the six-volume set of *World Poetry in Translation*. There was no question of bringing these upstairs: even if I had found somewhere to hide them, they would have been discovered. My mother had once discovered a West German comic book under Otto's mattress, and since then she had been in the habit of regularly turning the place upside down. I had brought a pencil and paper with me, my plan being to copy out one of the prose translations down here, and convert it into poetry upstairs. If anyone saw the copied-out translation, I would claim it was 'notes' for a poem.

With this in mind, I tipped one of the volumes to the light and began looking through it. I was searching for something that conformed in spirit to the quasi-abstract but unequivocally 'upward-aspiring' tenor of the artworks favoured in our home. I read quickly, aware that the longer I took, the more likely it was that I would have to account for my absence. Many years later, I heard a literature professor on the radio declare that the only valid criterion for judging a piece of writing was whether it could 'save your life'. Remembering my feverish ransacking of these volumes in the grainy darkness of the storeroom, I felt that I understood exactly what he was talking about.

I found what I was looking for, copied it out, put away the volumes and ran back upstairs, returning the key to Brandt.

Kitty was back. So, fortunately, was my mother, making it temporarily impossible for Kitty to question me about my alleged encounter with Jürgen. She gave me an anguished look, which I ignored. Just before dinner, I found her waiting for me as I came out of the bathroom. 'He wasn't there,' she whispered. I tried to look surprised. 'Maybe someone recognised him. He seemed nervous.' 'You said he looked –' Kitty managed, breaking off guiltily as my mother came out of the kitchen.

She regarded us a moment. The notion of Kitty and myself having any kind of relationship independent of the rest of the household, let alone something to whisper about, clearly both surprised and disturbed her. With a little movement at the back of her protruberant eyes, suggestive to me of a camera shutter opening and closing, she seemed to absorb the situation and store it away for further reflection, before ushering us on into dinner.

It was our custom to sit in the living room after dinner and listen to the latest instalment of one of the Russian novels that were continually being serialised on the radio. My father would sit back in his armchair with a glass of plum alcohol and pass into what seemed a state of innocent, genuine contentment. My mother fidgeted, torn between a sense that there might be something not altogether highbrow about this

42

method of ingesting culture, and the relish she took in telling people that this was how we passed our evenings as a family. (When she did this, she would deliberately stress the humble nature of the entertainment, implying, with her genius for suggestion, something simultaneously populist and austere in our tastes.) Perched restlessly on her chair, she would nod gravely at the passages of sententious generalisation, smile mysteriously at odd moments, as if to suggest an attunement to notes of humour too rarefied for the rest of us to catch, and sometimes sigh, 'Ah, yes,' apparently remembering a passage from her numerous readings of the book in her youth. Otto and I sat for the most part stupefied with boredom, though lately Otto had begun paying more attention. Since entering adolescence, he had made a private cargo cult out of any scraps of drama that could possibly be construed as erotic, hoarding them away for use in his private fantasies, and continually on the lookout for more. Kitty was seldom present: she usually went out in the evenings; if not, she stayed in her room.

That evening I announced that I would not be joining the family in the living room. I waited to be asked why, and with a joyful sense of importance answered that I needed to work on one of my poems. A bright, shining truth that seemed to bathe me in a fluorescent aura as I uttered it. I was immediately excused.

In my room, I took the prose translation from my pocket and set to work. The name of the poet I had stumbled on, and who, in the company of one or two others, was to prove so fatefully useful to me over the next few months, meant nothing to me at the time. But just as our janitor had for many years provided me with my mental image of the West German chancellor, simply because he bore the same name (leading to a great pang of bittersweet surprise when I first saw the exquisite, civilised, elfin face of Willy Brandt in the newspapers on the occasion of his momentous visit to Erfurt in 1970), so between Walt Disney (a controversial, if not actually unmentionable name at that time) and the word '*Witz*', meaning joke or wit, I formed the image of my stolen poetic persona as a kind of goofy, playful, disreputably capitalistic character. Though I couldn't read English, I had noticed that his lines were long, uneven and unrhymed. On a whim, I decided to reverse each of these qualities. Almost as soon as I began, I found myself strangely enjoying it – not that I discovered any great talent for producing short, regular, rhyming lines, but the very process of this weird inversion had a peculiarly natural, almost familiar feeling about it, as though I had already been doing it for years.

While I was happily working away, the door opened and Kitty came quietly into the room. Needless to say, she was after more information about her beloved Jürgen. What exactly did he say? What was his tone of voice? What had he been wearing? I sensed that she wanted the truth to match the romantic quality of her own feelings for the man. Since I was the sole source of this 'truth', I had it in my power either to bestow or to withhold what she wanted. It was unusual for me to find myself in a position of power over another human being. I was aware of it not so much in the Brandt sense of something to gloat over and exploit, as of a kind of transformative agent: a means of introducing a sudden and extreme volatility into a hitherto static situation. 'Well, his exact words were just, "Ask Kitty to come down and see me,"' I told her, 'but the way he said them was as though seeing you was the most important thing to him in the world.' I remembered she had knitted a red scarf for him, and I added that he was wearing that. A look of ardent longing came into her eyes. Gratitude also. She was perhaps twenty-six, not well educated, but in her quiet way fuelled by a passionate vitality that made her presence in a room always a positive enhancement. I knew that Otto had reassessed her lately from the point of view of his emerging sexuality, and found her to be desirable. As she looked at me, her eyes brightening with everything I said, I felt a kind of vicarious desire – as if I were Otto – and a corresponding rise in the value of the power I was wielding. Had I actually been Otto, I could surely have turned this situation to my advantage. Not least because Kitty, unsophisticated soul that she was, seemed at some level to be confusing me – the conveyor of pleasurable tidings – with Jürgen himself. For a moment the room seemed to brim with potentialities, as the two of us populated it with emblems of ourselves, each other, Otto and Jürgen, all conversing with one another. I felt that I was being given a foretaste of the world of adult passions, and a strong excitement came into me.

Footsteps approached. Kitty abruptly left the room. I heard my mother say 'Hello, Kitty,' in a bemused tone. She then appeared in my doorway.

'What are you and Kitty up to? You seem to be whispering like a pair of conspirators whenever I see you.'

She was smiling with her mouth open. She had two smiles: a close-mouthed smile for formal occasions, and an open-mouthed, vulnerably toothy smile for when she was being a mother on intimate terms with her children. I sensed, however, something duplicitous in her choice of smile now, as though she felt guilty about her compulsion to pry, or at any rate was trying to disguise it as innocent curiosity.

'What were you talking about?'

'Oh, nothing serious,' I said, racking my brains for something to tell her when she questioned me more forcefully, as I knew she would.

'Please tell me what you were talking about.'

'Kitty wants to knit something special for your birthday,' I managed to lie. 'She was asking me what I thought you would like.'

This silenced her for a moment. Seizing the advantage, I told her that Kitty had wanted the gift to be a surprise, and that now we had spoiled that. My mother looked uncomfortable, distressed even, and for a moment I felt an almost overwhelming urge to confess to all the absurd, trivial, but increasingly exhausting deceits her encouragement of my poetry had engendered.

'All right,' she said, 'we won't say a word to Kitty, and I'll act completely surprised on my birthday. Tell her to make me a matching hat, scarf and gloves. Blue, with white falcons on.'

And so that subsidiary chain reaction of unpleasantnesses finally petered out. Except that Kitty had to spend all her free time over the next few weeks knitting woollens for my mother.

MEANWHILE, the main sequence continued. The month passed, and preparations began for the next soirée. Eggs were hard-boiled and sprinkled with paprika. Chunks of canned Cuban pineapple were rolled in slices of ham. 'Plain, honest fare,' my mother would say as she served various combinations of these things. 'None of your Central Committee foie gras in *this* household.' As always in her assertions of humility, family self-esteem was maintained by the unstated, countervailing facts of the matter, which were that for most of our

46

visitors, even these relatively modest items represented a gastronomic treat.

It was November – windy and wet. Out of the bleary Berlin night guests began arriving, stamping their chilly feet in the hall, hanging their water-absorbent GDR raincoats on our iron coat rack.

I was in an agitated state. The idea of actually having to stand up in front of these people and reveal the fruits of my dubious labours was suddenly beginning to fill me with fear. For the first time it struck me that somebody might expose me as a fraud.

Uncle Heinrich hadn't arrived – his work often kept him late. I moved among the guests with waves of tension floating through my stomach. To my surprise, no one mentioned the performance they had made me promise to give. Either they had all forgotten, or – as I began to suspect – they had reached a tacit agreement among themselves to let the matter drop. Did they feel sorry for having pressured me? Or was it that they were really not very interested in hearing me read after all? Despite my anxieties, I found myself strangely resenting both of these possibilities. After an hour or so, I saw Uncle Heinrich's official limo – an old Czech Tatra – pull up on the street below. He came in, his usual kindly self, apologising for his lateness with a humility that never failed to flatter these people, any one of whom he could have destroyed with no more than his signature on a piece of paper.

He greeted me warmly, but he too failed to mention my promised reading. My deepening stage fright was compounded by a new anxiety, that I might not actually be called to the stage at all. The milk of human kindness may not have flowed in our household, but the milk of judicious approval for prowess in sanctioned fields could occasionally

47

be made to trickle. It was the only nourishment going, and I evidently thirsted for it.

Across the room I saw Franz Erhardt speaking with my uncle. I drifted over. Erhardt watched me approach, smiling thinly as I arrived, without pausing in his talk. I felt sure that he of all people could not have forgotten my reading, and was deliberately avoiding the subject out of professional rivalry. I could feel him willing me to leave, but I stood my ground. Eventually I looked at my watch and sighed so ostentatiously that they were obliged to notice.

'What is it, dear boy?' my uncle asked, concerned.

'Oh, nothing. Just that – well, I suppose I'm going to have to get those poems out. I've been dreading this.'

'Poems? Oh! Of course! Your reading!'

'I'd really rather not do it, Uncle Heinrich.'

'Nonsense! No backing down now!' He wagged a finger at me and summoned my mother over.

'Stefan promised to read to us. I'd quite forgotten. Now he's trying to wriggle out of it again.'

My mother looked at me. It seemed to me there was a little movement, a vague twinge of guilt, in the expressive depths of her eyes, as if she were at the point of supporting me in my alleged reluctance, as my father had the month before. Before she could speak, though, I shrugged my shoulders and said with an air of defeat:

'All right, I'll read them, if that's what you all want.'

I went to fetch the pages from my room. When I returned, the guests had been assembled in a circle around the piano, where Erhardt had read the previous month.

I had never addressed an audience before. My mouth had gone dry and my heart was pounding in my chest. The rows of people before me resembled nothing so much as the teeth of a gaping shark, ready to tear me apart. I wanted to flee from it, but it seems I also wanted to put my head in its mouth.

I managed to recite what I had written. The guests listened in silence, and when I finished there was applause.

For the record, the English equivalent of the lines I concocted would have sounded something like this:

> *I celebrate myself, myself I sing*
> *And my beliefs are yours, as everything*
> *I have is yours, each atom. So we laze –*
> *My soul and I – passing the summer days*
> *Observing spears of grass . . .*

And so on – an anodyne burble that was clearly too boring to raise suspicion. At any rate, nobody unmasked me.

But I realised almost as soon as it was over that not everything was as it had been before. The room may have been the same – the atmosphere of simulated conviviality certainly felt unchanged – but I myself was changed.

At first I didn't understand what had happened, but as the evening continued, with every guest obliged to make some kind of congratulatory remark, I realised that my attitude towards other people had undergone a radical alteration. Quite simply, the straightforward relation of cordial respect, or at least neutral interest, that is supposed to exist between people who have no prior reason not to respect each other was no longer available to me. It was gone, as if a cord had been cut. In its place, it seemed, was an intricately shuttling machinery of silent interrogation and devious concealment. Everyone I spoke to seemed newly illuminated by what I had done. Depending on certain minute signals given off by the movement of their eyes or the inflection of their voices (I felt suddenly attuned to these things), they were disclosed either as fellow hypocrites in whom the cord had also been cut (they had seen through my deception but weren't saying so), or else as innocent fools (they hadn't the guile to see through my deception). I was no doubt wrong in most of my individual diagnoses, but the idea that such a division might exist – between those in whom the cord has been cut, and those in whom it remains intact – was a revelation, and I still find myself appraising the people I meet on that basis.

My Uncle Heinrich, whose voluble enthusiasm for my performance led me to categorise him among the innocents, proposed that I should give another recital soon, since this one had been such a success. The proposal was immediately seconded by the person he was talking to, and by the logic of escalation that prevails in circumstances where power alone has meaning, someone else then had to suggest that I do it the very next month, only to have someone else trump them by saying I should do it *every* month. 'That way we'll all be able to witness first-hand the development of your young prodigy, Frau Vogel.' And before I knew it, I was looking at the prospect of my little act of stealth, which I had thought would now be cast off into the back-draft of history, having instead to be repeated, month after month after month.

There was one small upset before the soirée ended. A guest went into the bathroom and discovered Otto slumped on the floor, dead drunk. He had passed out while throwing up into the toilet.

Otherwise, the evening was considered a triumph, and for the next period of my life I devoted most of my energies to maintaining the façade of 'poet-intellectual' that my mother's warped pride had created and that I now began to half believe in myself.

It was a peculiar kind of drudgery – exhausting, depleting, and yet somehow compulsive. Like an inhabitant of hell – the hell of Sisyphus and Tantalus – I had a task, a labour, all of my own, and I felt inextricably bound to it. In its service life became a series of furtive routines. The stealing of the aquavit. The concealment of the theft. The bribing of Brandt. The removal of the key from his waist. The dark half hour in the storage room where I opened the trunk and copied the selected pages. The turning of the pages into 'poetry'. And then finally the nacreous glory of my monthly soul-bath in that crowd of admiring, captive faces.

A few years later, when I was making a private study of the career of Joseph Stalin, I came across descriptions of his seventieth birthday: the enormous portrait of him suspended over Moscow from a balloon, lit up at night by searchlights; the special meeting of the Soviet Academy of Sciences honouring 'the greatest genius of the human race' . . . The festivities culminated in a gala at the Bolshoi Theatre where the leaders of all the world's communist parties stood up one by one to make elaborately flattering speeches to Stalin, and lavish him with gifts. One can imagine his state of mind as he sat on the stage receiving these tributes – the absolute disbelief in the sincerity of a single word being uttered; the compulsive need to hear them none the less; the antennae bristlingly attuned to the slightest lapse in the effort to portray conviction . . .

It seems to me that at the age of thirteen, I had already developed the cynicism of a seventy-year-old dictator.

CHAPTER 3

One day I arrived home from school to find Otto remonstrating in a loud voice with my mother. I wandered into the kitchen, where the scene was taking place. Otto's broad, open face was a burning red colour. My mother was at her iciest.

'What I'm wondering is what kind of personal inadequacy this behaviour signifies. Perhaps it makes you feel more grownup to get drunk, is that it?'

'But I didn't do it!'

'It's a little pathetic, Otto, the thought of you sneaking in here to steal alcohol and then – what? – drinking it all alone under your blankets? Or is this what you do when you lock yourself in the bathroom?'

Otto flushed a deeper red. Although he had successfully defied my mother over the matter of becoming an artist, he still hadn't fully weaned himself of the need for her fundamental approval, which meant that he was still partly under her control. On her side, I think the threat of his independence of spirit made her more anxious than ever to test her power over him. She was constantly needling him at this time. Sometimes he would explode at her, as he had over the drawing classes, but more often he would simply come to a standstill, immobilised by a mixture of hurt, incomprehension and a need to be reinstated in her good opinion.

'It's also a bit unmanly. But perhaps you don't wish to grow into a real man. Perhaps you find the career of a social parasite more appealing? Do you? I ask because I assume you realise that that's where all this is leading . . .' The 'all' here derived from the fact that he had made himself sick with alcohol on two or three other occasions since the evening of my 'triumph'.

Otto's voice had grown strained, constricted. He gritted his teeth. 'I didn't *take* the aquavit. Somebody else must have taken it.'

I leaned against the enamel sink, observing. This was *my* life unfolding here, but it appeared to be doing so through the medium of someone else, as though it had acquired an existence separate from me.

'I see. You prefer to get someone else into trouble than face up to your own weakness. All right, let's hear it. Who would you like to accuse of stealing the bottles?'

'I don't know.' Otto glanced at me, then looked uncomfortably away. He shrugged.

'Stefan could have taken them just as easily . . .'

I said nothing. It was clear to me that I didn't need to object to this or deny it. My absolving was embedded in the logic of the scene, and required no contribution from me personally.

'Ah,' my mother said, 'I'm beginning to understand. You're suffering from jealousy of your younger brother. Well, well.'

'What? I'm just saying he *could* –'

'Correct me if I'm wrong, Otto, but I believe it was you who passed out drunk on the bathroom floor the night Stefan first read his poems? I've been trying not to regard that as an episode inspired by anything so petty-minded and bourgeois as envy. I hoped it might have been simple exuberance at your brother's success. But I see I must have overestimated your character.'

Otto blinked in a bewildered way, his large hands hanging helplessly at his sides.

'I . . . do . . . not . . . envy . . . Stefan!' He spoke thickly, as if from a deep fog of pain. I knew intimately what he would be feeling: the intolerable sense of injustice, the animal-like bafflement at his tormentor. It would be hypocritical to say that I was immune to the vague dispassionate satisfaction any child experiences at the chastisement of a sibling, but at the same time I could almost feel the lump that I knew to be thickening and welling in his throat, thickening and welling in my own.

'Perhaps it's my fault as a mother. Perhaps I should never have encouraged Stefan in his talent once it became clear that you were without talent. But notice how frankly I can speak to you about this. Do you understand why? Because your lack of talent has never made you a lesser person in my eyes. In your own eyes, perhaps, but in mine, no. We happen to be lucky enough to live in a society that values all individuals equally, provided they are honest and produc-tive, and I've always assumed anyone brought up in my household would have the intelligence to see that this was as true inside the home as out. Was I wrong, Otto? Have I made you feel less important than your brother? Is that why you stole from us? Please answer me. I'm trying to under-stand you. It may even be that I owe you an apology for overestimating your –'

And suddenly Otto did explode. Like a mad bull he threw himself around the kitchen, picking up plates and glasses and smashing them on the floor, all the while roaring wildly with rage. Casting about for something more spectacular to destroy, his eye lit on the instant coffee wireless my father had brought back from New York. Too status-rich to languish in the privacy of a bedroom, yet too obviously out of place in the living room, this now occupied a prominent shelf in the kitchen, visible from the corridor outside, the chrome letters of its maker's insignia always polished to a high gleam. Grabbing it from the shelf, Otto paused a moment, looking directly at my mother, as though waiting for a further signal from her before deciding what to do with this revered object.

'That, I think, is something you will regret breaking, Otto,' she said quietly, 'but go ahead, break it, if that's what you want to do. As I say, I assume you know where this is leading.'

Otto smiled and hurled the wireless to the floor, where the coffeemaking part of it broke into thick glass chunks. Then he charged out of the apartment, slamming the door behind him.

LATER THAT EVENING he was brought home by two cops in grey-green uniforms – *Volkspolizei*. My mother invited them into the living room. One of them hung in the doorway, overawed, it seemed to me, by the cultured atmosphere of the room – the book-lined shelves, the piano laden with scores, the mass of troubled but 'hopeful' semi-abstracts that had by now spread across the walls like some lurid fungal growth. The other officer came right in, however, his hand still proprietorially on Otto's arm, and sat down with Otto beside him, taking the measure of the place with a look of keen interest. His name was Porst. He had shining dark eyes, black hair, and a thin face that sagged here and there in little pouches.

From my point of view, the episode seemed to be occurring not so much in the physical space of the living room as in some lower depth of my own psyche. I felt it unfolding within me, but I felt nothing else – only a deepening of the numbness that had been with me since I had arrived home that afternoon.

It appeared that Otto had gone from our apartment to Mulackstrasse, a seedy part of town, where he had been able to buy a bottle of cheap vodka and drink himself into a stupor. The police had literally picked him up from the gutter. He would have been thrown into jail had Porst's compassion not been aroused. For one thing, Otto's papers showed that he was only fifteen. For another, he was carrying his membership card for the Free German Youth, the junior wing of the ruling Socialist Unity Party. I knew that Otto had joined them purely on account of the reputation of their mixed-sex summer camp, which he was hoping to attend this year, but Porst had taken it as evidence that Otto was at least not a complete degenerate, might even turn out to be fundamentally a 'sound lad', who perhaps, he suggested, would benefit more from some sharp discipline on the home front than a criminal charge of disorderliness.

'So what do you intend to do, Herr Vogel?' he asked my father.

'I – I don't know,' my father said helplessly. 'What do you suggest?'

'I think in a case of this seriousness, some physical element would be appropriate.'

My father looked stunned.

'You want me to beat him?'

Porst shrugged. 'It's up to you. We can take him back to the station if you prefer.'

'No, no,' my father said. 'Well . . . as you say, some physical element might not be inappropriate. Not now, of course, the boy's in no condition. Tomorrow morning, though, Otto. First thing.' He gave Otto a look intended to convey stern resolution. Otto gazed blankly back.

'Oh, I think now,' Porst said quietly. 'These things are best dealt with in the heat of the moment. Don't you agree, Frau Vogel?'

'I agree with you entirely,' my mother said. 'In fact, I was just telling my husband if he didn't take Otto in hand, we'd soon have a child with a criminal record. I must say, we're very lucky he ran into someone like you, though of course I know our police to be generally rather open-minded. My brother works in the Office of the Chief of the People's Police. Perhaps you know him? He's senior counsel there. Heinrich Riesen.'

'Yes, of course,' Porst said, visibly taken aback. There was a silence, during which the question of who was most at risk of 'receiving disadvantage' from the situation – now that my mother had unexpectedly dropped her brother's name in Otto's defence – seemed to debate itself almost audibly. It was Porst who finally backed down. With a sudden affable grin he turned to his colleague:

'Perhaps on second thought it's better for families to deal with these matters in private.'

The other man nodded with alacrity.

As they left, Porst pointed to the naked bronze lady in the corner of the room.

'That's a Kurt Teske, isn't it?'

'Yes, it is,' my mother replied. 'You know his work?'

'Oh, yes. I've been trying to get the department to buy one of his pieces for years. Well, goodnight.'

*

IN HER practical-minded way, my mother saw that she had pushed things too far with Otto, and that since there was probably nothing to be gained from further interference in his life, she might as well leave him to his own devices. She did this with an abruptness that left him at first disoriented, even upset, until he discovered he could survive very well without her intimate surveillance of his life.

Meanwhile, I became more than ever the apple of her eye. Into me she poured all her hopes and ambitions, her pride and her apparently insatiable appetite for glory. I became her knight-errant in the realm of artistic and intellectual endeavour, from which I was destined, we both believed, to bring back prize after prize. I am not sure what shape my ultimate success was to take – perhaps some lofty combined position at the Writers' Union, the Academy of Arts and various other of those spiritual crematoria in which the inner life of our republic was steadily being turned to ashes. Whatever it was, her hopes for me were so overwhelming that the lie on which they were founded often seemed to me merely a minor and really quite negligible detail.

It did, however, require maintenance. The young god had to show himself. He had to make his monthly appearance, his *theophany*, with a new token of his powers for his worshippers each time. For that he needed access to the trunk, and for *that* he had to have a bribe for Herr Brandt. The aquavit had been locked away, as I had known it would be the moment I heard my mother accuse Otto of stealing it. Throughout Otto's ordeal I had been wondering at the back of my mind what I was going to bring with me the next time I went down to the basement. I didn't have money to give Brandt, and I somehow didn't feel I would be able to secure his co-operation with a can of Cuban pineapple.

I went down empty-handed.

Far from feeling defiant, I remember a kind of looseness about me, as though I were in the process of surrendering to some large, dismantling power that had had designs on me for some time.

Brandt was in his glass-walled cubicle. He himself was asleep in his chair, but his scar, glittering crimson in the peculiar, poisonous-looking light that flickered between the neon ceiling halo and the green-painted walls, seemed wide awake. I had the impression that it was expecting me. The keys dangled from their ring, asprawl on Brandt's thigh, bobbing there as he breathed. A tight bud of anxiety was pushing up through my stomach. *Yes, yes, come in,* the bilious walls and the roil of glittering flesh seemed to whisper as I silently opened the door. *Yes, yes, very quietly, now.* But even as I crept towards Brandt, I knew that they had every intention of betraying me. I understood that what I was doing, as I ever so gently placed my fingers on the keys, was merely a kind of ceremonial formality, so that though it was physically a shock, it was in fact no great surprise when Brandt's heavy hand came down suddenly on mine. He held it first to the bunch of keys, then, sliding it with deliberately slow forcefulness (as if to demonstrate to me that we had now arrived in a realm where his power over me was absolute), he locked it onto his bulging groin. Barely deigning to open his eyes, he said, 'No more aquavit, eh?'

I nodded, and he, rousing himself from his chair, his hand still gripping mine, said, 'Come on, then,' and as if we had long ago agreed to this contingency, we went down together to the storage area, locking the door behind us.

*

59

I HAVE little graphic recollection of what I or Brandt actually did that afternoon or the afternoons that followed at monthly intervals. What survives in me more vividly than the physical details was the sense, already familiar to me at that age, that the harm being done to me had in some mysterious fashion already been done. *It had already happened.* Not literally, perhaps, but in a manner that made this manifestation of it little more than a kind of hieroglyphic record of an earlier, vaster event, as, say, a particular rock formation, made visible by a mudslide, records a seismic upheaval that took place in the earth's tectonic plates aeons ago. If there was any element of surprise, it was simply in the discovery that my blightedness was not by some miracle going to turn out to exclude this particular area of my being. But then I had had no reason to suppose that it would.

The other thing I remember is that Brandt never seemed to experience anything resembling pleasure during our encounters. The vacant look on his large, round face (the face of a baby left to bloat in a jar of formaldehyde) would turn actively gloomy when I arrived at his booth for the key now. As we walked in silence down the service stairway, I had the sense that he was moving there through the same miasma of dimly apprehended horror as I was, and as we groped and grappled lugubriously together in the near-blackness of the storage room, a pair of lobsters in a murky tank, he had the weary air of someone undergoing a peculiarly burdensome penance. I think of the paintings of Bosch – the demons as tormented-looking as their victims, the two at times barely distinguishable as they reach down into each other with the blunt instrument of themselves, entering and breaking. When it was over he would leave me to the privacy of my mother's trunk, limping off in a private cloud of muttered imprecations directed as much at the world in general as at me personally.

This state of affairs continued for perhaps a year. I was aware that it was unhealthy, to say the least, but at the same time it seemed inconceivable that it could be otherwise. It had come about by a process of invincible logic, one that I myself was complicit in, even if I hadn't initiated it, and for all its unwholesomeness, I recognised in its textures, its particular twists and turns, something that felt peculiarly *me*-like. I had created this strange, convoluted existence, as a sea creature creates the shell peculiar to itself. The distinguishing feature of this particular shell – to pursue the analogy – turned out to be its steady strangulation of its inhabitant. By the time I was freed from it, I was more dead than alive.

CHAPTER 4

Already largely absent from us in spirit, my father began to absent himself physically at this time. He let it be known at work that he was available for the least desired assignments, and began spending weeks at a time at convocations of minor functionaries in Sofia and Bucharest. My mother appeared not to notice, or at least not to mind, continuing indefatigably along the path she had chosen for herself. And then one day, when my father was away on one of his trips, she announced to us over dinner that he would not be coming back to live with us. He had fallen in love with another woman, she informed us drily, a colleague in his department. When he returned to Berlin he and my mother would be divorced, she told us, and he would be moving in with his colleague.

None of us had had any inkling of this, and we pressed my mother for more details, but she appeared to have taken the position that the event was nothing more than a minor annoyance, and the less said about it the better. Unsentimentality over matters of the heart was a point of pride among the educated classes in the former GDR, and my mother's behaviour was doubtless an attempt to prove herself a superior adherent to this code. It must have cost her something, though: when Kitty suddenly burst into tears at the table, my mother told her extremely sharply to stop. There was a moment's silence. Then her own eyes – to her apparent astonishment – filled with tears (the first and last time any of us beheld such a phenomenon), and she abruptly left the room. A stoical dryness was soon restored, however, and after that she contrived to give a characteristically lofty appearance of being above such commonplace emotions as wounded pride, petty vengefulness, or plain sorrow.

For the most part life continued unaltered after my father's departure, but there was one significant change. Although she may have considered it beneath her to display any personal response to the event, my mother seemed to feel that some kind of 'official' response was called for, just as a government is sometimes obliged to respond to some event its individual ministers are personally indifferent to, for the sake of the public's sense of balance. The response she settled on was a temporary suspension of her soirées. In this, as in all matters, there was no doubt a strategic motive: namely that their resumption, whenever it came, would be seen as a triumph over adversity. But whatever the case, I was abruptly liberated from my treadmill. No more fraught recitals, no more forgery, no more furtive dalliances with Brandt in the dark basement with its little mice and moths and beetles writhing and blinking on their glue traps all around us.

Suddenly, effortlessly, it was over. Almost too effortlessly, perhaps. With the feeling of a prisoner let out of his dungeon only to be told that the door had never in fact been locked, I drifted back up to the surface of my life, utterly bewildered.

Here, I discovered, things had been proceeding in quite momentous ways, apparently without need of my active participation. At school in particular, where I had been coasting for some time in a state of almost narcoleptic dreaminess, my life really did seem to have taken on a life of its own.

Ours was one of the elite high schools of Berlin, reserved for children of party officials. We had the best technical and athletic equipment, as well as the most highly qualified teachers, at our disposal, and it was expected that we would follow in the footsteps of our devout, industrious parents. Foreign and domestic dignitaries were constantly being wheeled into our morning assembly to impress on us the heroic nature of our destiny. Abrassimov, the Soviet ambassador, pinned Red Star badges on our chests one morning, carrying himself with the fantastical frostiness he was famous for, and that he evidently thought appropriate to his vice-regal status in our republic. Alexander Schalck-Golodowski came to talk to us about so-called 'German–German' relations. Erich Mielke, Politburo Member for Security, led us in our Pioneer Greeting one morning, before going on to address us on the joys of a career in counterintelligence. Guenter Mittag came to us from Economic Affairs . . . Illustrious names once; names to conjure with, their mere utterance sufficient to induce that sensation of awe reserved for remote, solemn powers – all gone now, disgraced, ridiculed, forgotten.

My mother's visit to my class at the time of our abortive move to New York turned out to have had one lasting effect: it had seriously compromised my position among my classmates. Although I hadn't been actively shunned, I had been put into a kind of social quarantine, a limbo-like condition where I was under close scrutiny pending the appearance of further symptoms that would indicate a full-blown case of unpopularity.

Unpopularity, as any schoolchild knows, is a highly specific spiritual sickness which can strike almost anybody at any given moment. It is as irrefutably real as the measles, and in its own way almost as contagious. Once a person has been diagnosed with it there is nothing he can do except wait patiently for it to run its course. Attempts to deny it or overcome it by ingratiating oneself with the uncontaminated will only result in ever crueller forms of rejection.

My fall from grace came about almost casually. One afternoon in summer, during our annual Hans Beimler athletic and paramilitary contests, I saw a group of my classmates sitting together on the grass of one of the playing fields. I had just won my quarterfinal in the two-hundred-metre dash, qualifying me for the next round, and I was feeling buoyant enough to join the group without being invited. They had been laughing, but by the time I joined them they had fallen quiet.

'Let's try it on Stefan,' somebody said. They had evidently been playing some game. I looked about cheerfully, always ready to offer myself as a source of entertainment.

A girl called Katje Boeden spoke. Katje was the daughter of a high-ranking official in Hermann Axen's Ministry of Foreign Affairs, and I had a private connection to her. A short time before my father's debacle in New York, her family had made a friendly overture to mine, and we had visited them at their house in the Wandlitz compound outside the city. It was a warm home, full of games and toys, and decorated with tribal art from Zanzibar, which gave it an almost bohemian flavour. Katje had been wearing a smocked green dress. On her blossoming body it had seemed to gather up all the innocent wonder of childhood and draw it surreptitiously into a strange new context – that of imminent sexual awakening. The effect on me had been powerful. While Otto went off with her older brother Paul, she took me into the garden where

65

she had a tree house in a half-dead beech tree. We sat talking for what seemed hours – about what, I have no recollection, but I was bewitched by her. Unfortunately, my father lost his job soon after, and our visit was neither returned nor repeated.

Over the next two or three years, Katje had grown extremely pretty – petite, with sharp, delicate features, sparkling blue eyes and fair hair which she wore in a tight, gleaming crown of braids. Though she never made any reference to our meeting at her home, she was always friendly towards me.

'Name the first three animals to come into your head, Stefan,' she said.

I forget the first two animals I named, but the third was the three-toed sloth. After a pause there was a titter of laughter: gentle enough at first. Conscious of being a good sport, I sat with my smile, waiting for an explanation. But as the merriment seemed about to subside, a peal of louder, more fulsome and somehow more ominous-sounding laughter broke from Katje. For several seconds it sounded out alone; clear and pure, like the clarion call announcing the arrival of a new force into the field. Then one by one the others joined in, and suddenly they were all doubled up with the kind of wild, hysterical, self-perpetuating laughter that teenagers everywhere so enjoy being overcome by. I continued smiling, telling myself there was nothing to be dismayed about, and yet feeling a faint ache in my throat, and sensing, distantly, the advent of something momentous and catastrophic.

'The first animal is how you see yourself,' a boy told me when the group had begun to calm down, 'the second is how others see you. And the third is what you really are.'

'A three-toed sloth,' Katje shrieked, and once again they were shaking their sides and rolling on the grass, helpless with laughter.

A day or two later, during a geography class, where we were giving presentations on the tropical zone, a boy stood up and announced with a sly grin that he was going to talk about the three-toed sloth. I would say that my heart sank, except that 'sank' implies a depth of plummeting that wasn't quite what I experienced. Rather, my heart slid down a little, then seemed to move more in a sideways direction, so that as I heard the boy inform us that a sloth stays so still that mould grows in its hair, that its maximum speed – that of a mother sloth hurrying to protect her child – is five metres per hour, that they aren't hunted because even when shot dead they continue clinging to their branch, not dropping until they reach an advanced state of decomposition, and so on, while smiles danced about the room like little sunbeams, what I felt was not some ever-blackening descent into misery, but more a kind of anaesthetising removal, as if I were travelling out beyond the walls and windows towards some point of absolute detachment and indifference. I saw that I had fallen from favour, and I accepted this without protest – inward or outward. After all, I told myself, feeling my familiar sense of *déjà vu*, this had *already happened*. It had happened long ago: what had just occurred was no more than a case of fallible human judgement belatedly recognising the verdict handed down against me long ago by some impassive agency of reality itself.

The last athletic qualifying rounds were held on a sweltering, overcast afternoon. The acrid smell from the chimneys of the nearby foundries and breweries was particularly heavy in the air. I sat on a bench alone, waiting for the semifinals of the two hundred metres. Though I wasn't what you would call an athlete, I had always been able to cover short distances at above-average speed. I relate this faculty directly to my ability to think up ingenious falsehoods at short notice. Both have to do with the instinct for evasion, which has always been more highly developed in me than that of confrontation. As I sat on the bench I fantasised about winning my round and then going on to win the final itself the following week. In my vision, my face remained stern as I crossed the finishing line, as though to convey that I scorned any hope that this victory might alter my status as an outcast. But as I left the field I would catch Katje's eye, and although she would say nothing, the brief stalling of her attention would tell me that a secret connection had been opened up, linking her in her realm of light to me in my darkness.

In reality what happened was this: As soon as the starter pistol was fired and I leaped forward with my rivals, I became aware of something that at first presented itself as a kind of abstract sense of obstruction. Normally when I ran this race I would have the pleasurable sensation that it was somehow tailor-made for my own particular combination of skills, stamina and ambitions. But now I felt unexpectedly at sea. My body didn't seem to know what to do. Instead of obediently turning itself into an instrument for the expression of speed, it seemed to want to express some new idea of doubt or faltering. I felt that I wasn't so much running as flailing. After a moment I realised that among the shouts coming from the spectators lining the track were cries of unmistakably hostile intent. 'Five metres per hour,' I heard, 'There's mould growing on your fur,' and 'You're decomposing, Vogel.' It was these cries that were thickening the air about me. If ever I wanted proof of the communist idea of the individual as a social unit, even to his physiological functions, I had it here: the sense of my comrades actively willing me not to win the race was indeed slowing me down, their words dragging on my limbs like lead weights. I caught sight of Katje up ahead of me, thronged by her companions. As I drew level with her, I heard her cry out, her delicate-featured head tilted back in an attitude of ecstatic contempt, 'Here comes the three-toed sloth.' The space about me felt almost viscous, the sour-ochre smell of burnt malt and coal dust mingling and merging with the hatred radiating towards me, each somehow amplifying the other, until I felt suffocated and nauseous. As I moved slowly across the finishing line, several metres behind the slowest of my rivals, I found myself panting for air and strangely dizzy. Suddenly the ground swung up towards my face and I blacked out.

When I came round (I had fainted, apparently from heat exhaustion), I understood that my long quarantine was over. The worst had been confirmed and I was now officially unpopular.

From this time forth I was referred to as 'Sloth' or 'Three-toed Sloth', and I was considered fair game for all the ambient spite and aggression that gusted about the school to vent itself on. My life became highly unpredictable. For days on end I might be totally ignored. And then suddenly, out of nowhere, a storm of the most violent hostility would erupt about me. I would find myself being shoved and kicked, my books being torn from me and thrown all over the place, my nickname being chanted with the peculiar gleeful derisiveness (like the ecstasy I had noted on Katje's face) that appeared to be one of the distinguishing features of my persecution. After a few weeks, as though the virulence of my case weren't sufficiently expressed by these manifestations, there was a further development. It took the form of a sign: an oval paw shape, with three clawlike protruberances. It appeared first on the toilet doors, then spread rapidly throughout the school, showing up on chalkboards, official notice boards, desktops, even the classroom walls themselves. At first I attempted to erase these sloth paws whenever I saw them, but for every one I removed, another dozen would appear, and I realised this was futile. Besides, there was a sense in which I regarded them as having emanated from *myself*, rather than my comrades. They were the proliferant, bitter fruit of a tree that had its roots in my own being. For not only was it I who had delivered into my comrades' hands the fateful image of the sloth in the first place, but it was also my own compromised condition as a human being that had made them so ready to seize on it and use it as a weapon against me.

At that time of collective sexual burgeoning, it was clear to me that I had allowed something poisonous to enter into this most sensitive part of myself, and in doing so to canker it. I awoke from my wet dreams feeling more anxious than gratified, my head suffused with a sickly afterglow left behind by apparitions whose superficial femininity could never quite conceal some underlying nuance or redolence of Herr Brandt. In those unenlightened times, the obtrusion of such a figure into one's erotic dream life was alarming, to say the least.

My daytime fantasies were similarly contaminated. At first these invariably featured Katje, with whom I continued to imagine, pathetically but ardently, situations in which a 'secret connection' would suddenly be revealed between us. In absolute silence we would withdraw from the outer world where she was obliged to keep up the appearance of my tormentor, into a private realm of sharply enhanced intimacy in which her true feelings for me spilled out in waves of intense, radiant warmth. There, we would hold hands, looking tenderly into each other's eyes. I would kiss her lips, feel her small mouth yield beneath mine, and taste the sweetness of her tongue. Drawing back a moment, she would look at me almost pleadingly, as though begging my forgiveness for all the spitefulness she was obliged to heap on me in the outer world. Shyly she would remove her blouse, offering me her girlish breasts with their budlike nipples. As I kissed them, I would reach a pitch of arousal. And then suddenly Brandt would appear in my mind, a ponderously scoffing presence, his face wearing that old knowing sneer, as though to say, *Who do you think you're fooling?* And with an inward slump, I would feel the burden of my contagion, my brokenness, reassert itself inside me, and my brief, celestial vision would dissolve.

Given its physical effects, it was not surprising that this burden should assume a physical form in my imagination. The image that would come into my mind was Brandt's scar. I began to feel as though that snail trail of glistening scarlet tissue had migrated from him to me, and that although it might not be visible to the eye, its presence upon me was nevertheless clear as day. This was why people had begun to recoil from me, and it seemed to me entirely natural that they should do so. I remember that whenever I was attacked, whether verbally or physically, a part of me was always firmly on the side of my attackers. If it had been possible to divide myself in two, I would probably have joined them in their assaults on me.

I had already tasted the paralysing effects of this antagonism during my two-hundred-metre semifinal. What happened to me over the next few years, as my unpopularity ran its course, was essentially an enormously drawn-out version of precisely that experience.

A deep lethargy settled on my spirit. My mind grew dull and my body felt permanently torpid. I began to see the requirements of my life in terms of immeasurable distances that had to be crossed, but never could be, so infinitely slow had I become, so that it was better not to embark on them at all. At home I spent hours at a time horizontal on my bed. I would like to say that I became self-scrutinising and studious, that I read copiously, read 'everything', but in truth I spent most of the time staring at the ceiling. If I did develop any form of connoisseurship, it was a connoisseurship of vacancy. I retain from that period the sense of a mysterious relationship between rooms and time. At a certain depth of immobility one forgets the ostensible function of a room as a shelter or area boxed off for some specific activity, and begins to experience it in its purer nature, as a ship transporting one across the ocean of time. The more motionless I became, the more apparent was this function. At times it seemed to me I could almost feel the slight swell and surge of that invisible element beneath me, and this was a strangely pleasurable sensation – a feeling of naked contact with a mighty power intent on annihilating everything and fully capable of doing so. I told myself that I need only lie there and let myself be carried forward for every vexing thing that surrounded me to fall away and crumble into dust. That I myself would be a part of this slow-motion Armageddon was merely an added bonus.

My lethargy thus fed on itself, growing thicker and heavier, until I reached the point where even the simplest, most basic tasks, such as opening a window or closing a door, would have to assert their demands on me with an irresistible urgency, before I could stir myself to perform them.

During this period I formed the idea that every phenomenon that comes into being represents a victory in a struggle against a force willing it *not* to come into being. I pictured this opposing force as a kind of Chinese Dragon, a Dragon of Stability, jealously guarding the status quo. It patrolled the borders between occupied and unoccupied space, and it lay curled and scowling at the threshold of every possible action. In order to open a window one must first slay the dragon posted to ensure that the closed window remain for ever closed. The fire these dragons breathed took the form of waves of paralysing intertia, a breath of which was enough to overcome you unless you had extraordinary vitality as well as unshakeable belief in the importance of what you wanted to do. More and more I found myself defeated before I could even move. Was it worth the almighty struggle, the expenditure of limited energy, to open that window, when after all nothing material would be changed by doing so, and when, even if I succeeded, another dragon would immediately be posted to ensure that the now-open window would now remain for ever open? Increasingly, it seemed not.

In this way the dragons grew steadily bolder and more numerous, crowding into the most intimate corners of my existence, until I could almost see them, massed about me like iguanas I had seen in pictures of the rocks of the Galapagos Islands, fatly luxuriating in the near-perfect stultification they had finally procured.

The only thing that punctuated my inertia was an occasional bout of yearning. Yearning is the passive form of protest: instead of trying to change things by a concrete attack on what exists in the here and now, it puts its faith in what lies beyond. The objects that triggered this feeling varied, but they had in common a mixture of enchantment and a kind of shyness, an inclination to retreat or disappear from view.

I became susceptible to certain aspects of the natural world for the first time. Nature impinged very little on our life in

Berlin, but that made the occasions when it did all the more piercing. A group of slender trees, greyish with a dim, pewter-like gleam and fine raised lines shoaling horizontally around the smooth skin of their trunks, rose from the rubble of a derelict public garden near our apartment. They were grouped closely, in a way that stressed their kinship and gave them the appearance of conversing with each other, in a language known only to themselves. That and the slight glimmering sheen of their barks gave them a mysterious glamour in my eyes. They seemed to be concealing a vivid, secret life of their own. I would stop and look at them, mesmerised by the vague suggestion they gave out, of a realm of existence contiguous with mine, yet utterly unlike it. I yearned to cross the threshold into this realm, to reconfigure myself within its matrix of sap, fibre and sunlight, and there were times, stilling myself to the utmost, when I felt on the point of doing so, whereupon, as though suddenly aware of being encroached on, the trees would abruptly withdraw into themselves, becoming mute, inert, wooden. Likewise with the sky. Mostly it was grey, but sometimes on winter afternoons, as the sun went down behind the great apartment blocks that marched to the farthest horizon in every direction, it would turn a clear amethyst colour, and things that were not noticeable before were briefly inscribed in fire: strange runes, hairpins, chunks of frozen drapery, cat's paws of dispersing jet vapour; suggestive of the traffic of other empires, parallel with and utterly unlike our own; infinitely beguiling and absolutely elusive.

That which withholds itself came to form my definition of the desirable. Most of the girls at my school came into this category. Katje's successor in my imagination was a Russian girl named Masha, the daughter of a visiting physicist. She had dark, glistening hair and a smooth, dark-complexioned face with narrow green eyes that turned delicately upwards at the outer corners, giving her a look at once feline and oriental. She was extremely reserved; probably just shy among her new companions, but I chose to attribute it to an innate sense of superiority over us benighted locals. Our German tongue in her Soviet mouth became strangely transformed, the vaunted exactnesses of its agglomerate noun phrases melting back from pure, harsh meaning to something almost music-like as she blithely softened every vowel and liquefied each consonant. On the rare occasions when she condescended to speak in class, I would listen to her with a feeling of anguished desire. Like the trees and the sunset-lit clouds, she gave the impression of being merely the outermost flourish of some immense, hidden universe, and her voice, making sounds that were simultaneously familiar and alien, seemed the point of entry. We never exchanged a word or even a look, but unknown to her she and I conducted a prolonged, passionate love affair. In the private theatre of my psyche, I took her on long walks through the city, glutting myself on the erotic melancholy of her presence, kissing her fervently in the drizzle under budding linden trees, taking her invisibly home to my bed and murmuring her name over and over until I had worked myself into a state of rapture. She disappeared from our midst as unexpectedly as she had arrived. But such was the perverse premium I now put on unattainability that the effect was merely to intensify our relationship, enshrining her in my imagination with the solid gold burnish of an icon from her native land.

And then finally there were the things my father had brought back from America – my Slinky, my diver's watch, my skyscraper pens. Having neglected them for a while, I once again found myself gratefully appreciating these objects. I pored over them, feeling them dilate in my mind until the world they connoted – snatches of imagined music, imagined flavours and textures, intimations of freer, larger human types – was more vividly present to me than my own surroundings.

One of the advantages of living on our side of the Wall was our ability to believe that happiness did actually exist somewhere on earth, namely in the West. Happiness had a home. For most of my compatriots the name of that home was West Germany, and its furnishings were the products they saw advertised on the West German shows they tuned in to nightly on their TVs – the laundry soaps and detergents whose accompanying celestial and erotic imagery brought home so forcibly the terminal shittiness of our own *Spree* and *Dega*. But I seemed to have inherited my mother's instinct for the deeper hierarchies – either that or my father's aborted career had made more of an impact on me than I had realised: for me the name of that home was always America. In an obscure, private, but crucial sense, the trees I stared at were American trees, the clouds in the amethyst sky were American clouds, Masha was as American, despite her ostensible Russianness, as my father's souvenirs. Although I wasn't conscious of harbouring a wish to 'go to America', it strikes me that these acts of passive contemplation, of yearning, were perhaps not so different from the rituals of primitive hunters, who feel it necessary to take possession of their quarry in their imaginations before they can hope to do so in the flesh.

CHAPTER 5

'The rib's OK – just badly bruised. But do you see this?'

The emergency room doctor looked at me with a mixture of concern and professional excitement. He had clipped the X-ray to a light box on the wall, giving me a monochrome view of my own rib cage and cloudy interior.

'This whiter spot here . . .' Pointing between two spectral ribs. 'I can't say for sure, but I think we may be looking at an early stage of pulmonary tuberculosis.'

I followed the finger to what did seem a solider brightness in the blurred milky webbing to the right of my spine.

'The bacillus leaves calcium in the tissue, which shows up harder than other kinds of scarring. This is hard, though it's small still. My guess would be that you haven't felt any symptoms yet. Any blood in your spit?'

'No.'

'Sore throat? Persistent cough? Weight loss?'

'No.'

'I didn't think so. Well, I can't say for sure till we do a sputum culture, but I must tell you this looks like classic TB shadowing here.'

'I thought TB had been wiped out.'

'Well . . .' A young man with the wispy beard and palely burning eyes of a *Wandervogel* in photos from the twenties, except that a shifty movement in them now suggested someone after all not so unfallen: 'You're right, of course, it *has* been wiped out here in the GDR, but we do occasionally see a case of, well, *foreign* infection.' A man in whom, like me, the cord had been prematurely cut. 'Have you travelled abroad? I mean, to the West?'

'No.'

'Other members of your family?'

I shrugged – or rather, animated the shrug that by now resided permanently in my shoulders.

'My father used to travel to New York.'

'New York? I think we need look no further.'

'That was several years ago.'

'Yes, well, this could easily be an old infection, recently activated, assuming it *is* TB, which I don't want to say for certain at this stage . . .' He eyed me intently – trying, I sensed, to rouse me to a more appropriate level of anxiety, or at least curiosity, about my possible plight, than I was showing.

'What happened, by the way? The nurse said you'd had some sort of accident? A fall or something?'

'I was running down some stairs,' I told him. 'I tripped on a loose stone and just – went flying.'

He gave me a look that may or may not have had the Brandtian sneer of scepticism I projected into it.

'That's all?' His eyes seemed to flicker briefly over my throat.

'Yes.'

His interest in the circumstances of my arrival at the hospital, where I had taken myself after two days of privately endured pain, thinking I had broken my rib, was probably without ulterior motive. But by that point in my life – I was seventeen – concealment had become second nature to me.

78

A nurse took a sputum sample. Two weeks later I was informed that tubercule bacilli had been cultured from the sample, and that I should report directly to the hospital, to commence treatment.

So. I had become sick. Quite possibly, I had been sick for some time; sick with something to my ear unequivocally fatal-sounding. It was curable, of course, and the doctor who took charge of my case had no doubt that I would make a full recovery, but this fact seemed to me a minor detail in the overall picture the diagnosis presented to my imagination. This was one of the great annihilating instruments by which nature periodically winnowed out certain forms of weakness from the human species. In identifying me as a bearer of this weakness, she had confirmed a sense that had been growing in me over several years: the sense that I was, to all intents and purposes, already dead.

I went for my examination every week at first, then every month. My temperature was taken. I was weighed. A nurse stuck a clean cardboard tube into a spirometer. I blew into it while the stylus recorded my lung capacity on the revolving drum of graph paper. From the nurse's room I drifted somnambulistically on towards the deeper and denser space of the X-ray room. In a cubicle with a poster of Erich and Margot Honecker greeting the Ceausescus outside the Kremlin, I removed my school shirt and jacket, then stepped into the chamber itself, where the radiologist fastened a lead girdle about my waist to protect my seed, my orange seed, then positioned me against the backing plate, angling my shoulders forward to touch the cold metal. 'Now take a deep breath,' she would say, at which, with a soft buzzing sound like the perpetual buzzing in my own ear, the rays would probe into me.

I felt as if I had gone back underground, back to the place of obligatory yet never fully explicable rituals that I had submerged myself in during my storage room phase, repetition once again endowing each stage with a gloomy ceremoniousness. After the X-ray, the forty-minute wait in the passage outside the changing cubicles. Waste bins overflowing with phlegm-sodden tissues. Metal chairs attached to the linoleum – *bolted* to it, as though a weakness in the lungs had been found to predispose a person towards chair theft. Then a summons down a further set of corridors to a small waiting room, the antechamber to the offices of the physicians themselves. Quieter here; silent, in fact; the silence of thought finally undistracted from mortality – the contemplation of an emphysema here, a pleurisy there, there a lung cancer. My name was called and I walked to the numbered room where my physician awaited me – not the young emergency room doctor but an older man, Dr Serkin, an enigmatic person whom I lacked both the means and the will to understand at the time, and whom even now I find difficult to bring into clear focus.

He was about sixty. Sixty during the seventies, which meant already twenty and thirty during the thirties and forties. A survivor, then; veteran of the nazification, the denazification, the Marxist-Leninisation of his profession. At first his manner was distant, with the remote, deliberate calm of someone practised in the art of inward emigration. I associated him with the machines – the ancient, cumbrous, beige-enamelled machines – that stood about in the various rooms I passed through on my way to his. He seemed to aspire to their condition of imperturbability, and he projected something of their contained, humming power.

'Come in. Sit down.'

I sat beside him at a table under the mounted light box. My case notes lay open on the table. Beside each entry was a small pictogram of my lung, which Dr Serkin drew meticulously each week in turquoise ink, with arrows pointing to a mark that represented the infected patch.

'How do you feel today?'

'All right.'

'Still orange?'

'Yes.'

'How many of me do you hear at the moment?'

'Just one.'

'Any buzzing?'

'All the time.'

He glanced at the notes.

'Here – do you see something?' Pulling out a blank sheet of paper, he thrust it towards me. A bluish radiance quivered briefly across the white surface.

'Yes.'

Having felt no symptoms of the illness itself, I was now suffering in numerous ways from its cure. The dense orange capsules of isoniazid I took every morning dissolved in my system like blocks of indelible dye, staining all my bodily fluids an unnatural sunset colour that made me feel like a creature from another planet whenever I sweated or ejaculated. Overstressed by the toxicity of the pills, my liver sent thick drifts of floaters up across my visual field. Sometimes when I looked at a blank sheet of paper I saw palpitations of blue light flicker off the whiteness. My hearing too had been afflicted: a sound like the roll of a soft, insistent snare drum played continuously in my left ear. Occasionally a single voice addressing me would refract into a whole chorus of voices, all declaiming the same words like a massed, menacing choir.

Strange as they were, these phenomena seemed to me entirely natural: it was fitting, somehow, that a dead person should see the world of the living through a veil of swarming small print, hear it through a perpetual buzzing or rustling in one ear. Even now, when I learn of a death, the image that comes into my mind is of the deceased person suddenly thrust into a realm where the inhabitants all suffer from acute tinnitus and weep fluorescent orange tears.

In his remote fashion, Dr Serkin seemed to find these side effects amusing, or at least intriguing, and by association I myself seemed to grow fractionally more interesting in his eyes. As the weeks passed, I sensed a distinct desire on his part to communicate. His habit of mind was apparently such that anything he wished to say had to negotiate its way through a labyrinth of defensive caution, and consequently tended to come out in the form of odd little non sequiturs or else remarks too elliptical or ironic for me to fathom. Not that I was interested in doing so, any more than I was in his more direct attempts to make me open up about myself; an attitude that in retrospect I regret, as I suspect now that he was trying to help me.

After the questions about my side effects, he would exchange his look of private amusement for a more business-like expression, gesturing at me to remove my shirt so that he could begin the painstaking auscultations that preceded the examination of the X-ray. I sat there passively while he tapped and thumped me, listening through his stethoscope to the secret, involuntary confessions of my body. Once, while he was doing this, he began to question me quite insistently:

'So you thought you'd broken a rib? That's what brought you to the hospital?'

'Yes.'

82

'Fell down some stairs or something?' Tap-tap-tapping my sternum.

'Yes.'

'How?' Inching the cold stethoscope across my chest.

'I was running. I tripped.'

'That's all?'

'There was a loose stone.'

'It's interesting that your heart starts pounding like a jack-hammer when you tell me this.'

He glances at me. His eyes are large and distantly kind. Unillusioned, but without cynicism. Cord intact. Taking my X-ray from its folder, he clips it to the light box and puts the previous week's X-ray up beside it for comparison, switching on the light.

'The duty doctor who admitted you mentioned he'd noticed abrasions around your throat. What would that have been from?'

'I don't know.'

'Was somebody trying to strangle you?'

The choral effect kicks in.

'No.'

'None of my business, eh?' Fifty voices interrogating me in unison. Commas and colons raining in thick squalls across my eyes . . . I dispense a shrug, saying nothing.

'By the way, you have an unusually large lung capacity. Did you know this?'

'No.'

'In the old days that would have been seen as the sign of a tremendous *élan vital*.'

Sullen monosyllable from the patient.

'Which was not unreasonable, given that the oxidation of tissue is the basis of life, and that the lungs provide the means

83

for that oxidation. Would you say that describes you, an unusual vitality? Stefan?'

'I don't know.' Withdrawing into the tightest corner of myself.

'It's true, you seem more a Werther type than a Mynheer Peeperkorn . . . But on the other hand . . . well . . . under certain circumstances certain qualities take the form of their opposite. Like a tarot card upside down. Only sometimes it's the context that's upside down, not the card, if you take my meaning. I assume they teach you the tarot at school?' A sudden sardonic glimmer; it and the words themselves vectoring on a point too remote from my frame of reference for me to locate.

'No.'

'What are your plans in life, Stefan?'

'I don't know.'

'I had a son a few years older than you. An engineer. He wanted to design a car. A *fast* car. A beautiful fast machine for travelling on the open road. By which he did not mean a new-model Trabant on the Allied Transit Route.' He gives a dry, violent laugh. 'And by the tarot, *I* mean of course the socialist tarot. The Theoretician. The Party Chairman. The Enemy of the People. The Hanged Comrade. That's one for you, perhaps, Stefan?'

I see myself beside him at the table, my guard too firmly up against further questioning to take in anything he might be trying to convey to me, let alone anything instructive in the sight of my own rib cage hanging luminously before me on the light box. And I see Dr Serkin peering at the two images, *into* them, rather, as if he were staring into deep space. The ethereal skeins of tissue, the ghostly vein branches outlining the lungs' lobules of infundibula, look like maps of the heavens, full of star clusters, strange nebulae, hazy auroras. Closing one eye, the doctor holds his pen up to each X-ray in turn. With his air of powerful, suppressed disquiet, he seems less like a doctor than a tutelary spirit, trying to lead a reluctant initiate to the brink of some new realm of knowledge. A *Fluchthelfer*.

'What happened? Did you try to hang yourself?'

'No!'

From a tree in an old quarry in Friedrichshain, Dr Serkin. Overlooking the Spree River. A birch tree with its own diseased core; a rotten branch that broke when I jumped. I didn't know then that a birch among taller trees was more than likely to be dead; light-starved, decaying from within. I fell onto my back, then the heavy branch, still roped to my neck, came crashing down onto my rib. Not so much a Werther type as a circus clown.

'Well, anyway,' says the doctor, '*Felix culpa*. Isn't that what they say? Lucky fall? I mean, if you hadn't fallen, you wouldn't have found out about the TB – perhaps until it was too late.'

You mean if I hadn't tried to kill myself, I might have died? Is that what you were telling me, Dr Serkin?

He never mentioned his son again, and I never asked what had happened. One has to feel vaguely human oneself before one can start caring about other humans. *Sorgen*: to care; so much more absorptive, somehow, of the world's sorrows than the English word, but not a part of my active vocabulary before I met Inge.

CHAPTER 6

Speaking of feeling human, it is now the moment for me to say a few words about our 'lodger', Kitty.

Katerina Rust (to give her her full name) was the daughter of a serving girl, Lotte Rust, who had spent most of her short life on the estate of my mother and uncle's family near Breslau, in Silesia.

During the war Lotte and my mother stayed together at the house (a small castle, by all accounts), which was turned into a convalescent home for wounded officers. When the Red Army arrived on German soil and the Reich began falling into the pandemonium that preceded its final collapse, the two women, both still in their teens, fled west together, preserving, by mutual agreement – so my mother claims – the hierarchy of their relationship through thick and thin, surviving refugee camps, marauding troops from General Chuikov's army, cold, hunger and numerous other indignities arising out of our nation's unappreciated attempt to spread the gift of itself to the rest of the world. After the dust settled, they found themselves reunited with Heinrich (who had served in the army) in Soviet-occupied Berlin.

It seems Lotte was an attractive woman. She formed a liaison with a young Russian Comecon officer, a connection that gave the new household definite advantages in terms of political protection and basic necessities. The affair ended abruptly when the officer was posted back to Moscow, leaving Fräulein Rust heartbroken, and pregnant with Kitty. She died of diphtheria when Kitty was six, entrusting the girl's upbringing to my mother, who fulfilled the obligation in her own fashion. When I was very young, I thought of Kitty as my older sister, but as I grew up I saw that her status in our household wasn't after all quite that of a fully paid-up family member. Though she was fed and clothed as well as the rest of us, and though there was never any mention of anything so vulgarly uncommunist as servants or mistresses, there seemed to be an understanding between her and my mother that she was to perform all the more menial of the house-hold chores. It was Kitty who swept and dusted, who oper-ated the People's Own Washer we proudly purchased in the sixties, hooking its hose up to the kitchen sink and standing guard for the hour and a half it took to heat up (someone had to be there in case its gaskets burst); Kitty who served the titbits at my mother's soirées, Kitty who was sent out to stand in line for bananas or toothpaste or the cans of *Schmalzfleisch* my father liked to have on his toast for break-fast. She never complained or showed any sign of resenting her position; in fact, she seemed deeply attached to us all, and strangely devoted to my mother, as though she had inher-ited her own mother's accommodating humility.

Humble, yes, and passionate too. The slightest emotional tremor would widen her flecked grey eyes and bring a flush of colour to her pale cheeks. Though she claimed to be intim-idated by the 'intellectual' tone of our home, and would often describe herself (with curious relish, it struck me) as an 'igno-ramus' or even an 'idiot', she had more real curiosity than any of us. She read voraciously – novels, plays, art history, books about ancient civilisations; anything she could get her hands on. Always, I discovered, with the sense that she wasn't quite getting the point, wasn't enough of an intellectual 'like you or your mother' to penetrate into the grand revelations about the meaning of life that she was certain lay concealed beneath the surface of the text. She left school at sixteen and apprenticed at a state garment factory, meaning to take her *Abitur* and go on to a technical institute to learn apparel design, but getting sidetracked instead – into clerical work, administration, bouncing from one secretarial post to another, her neat and pretty appearance keeping her dependably in new bosses whenever she needed a change. And like many people I have met whose buoyant disposition and natural charm should have ordained them, by the laws of nature itself one would think, for a life of uncomplicated happiness, she seemed instead to be doomed to one of serial disappointment and devastation. One after another the men she fell in love with turned out to be shits, thugs, liars or, as in the case of the aforementioned Jürgen, outcasts who could offer her little more than a fleeting, anguished memory of themselves. A recurring motif during my adolescence was the sight of her at the kitchen table, weeping beside my mother, who would offer a selection of dry observations about the man in question and reprove Kitty for her poor judgement. Stony consolation, yet it seemed to be all Kitty wanted, or at any rate felt she deserved.

At one point, some time in her twenties, she made a determined effort to take herself in hand. She got a place to study textiles at a vocational school in Leipzig – a three-year programme that would lead to the *Abitur* and then, if she was lucky, to university.

After a few months in Leipzig she got involved with a

chemistry teacher who turned out to be married with three children. As soon as she discovered this, Kitty tried to break off the relationship, but the teacher declared himself to be unable to live without her, and at the same time threatened to orchestrate her expulsion from the school if she stopped sleeping with him. Confused and frightened, she allowed herself to be blackmailed in this way for several months, aware of a gathering tide of disapproval moving towards her from all quarters, as word of the affair got out. Finally she received a visit from the leadership of the school branch of the FDJ, who monitored, among other things, the development of 'socialist personality' in the student body, and put it to her that she might benefit from some serious re-education in this department. A week later, distraught, ashen, her eyelids puffy and scarlet-rimmed from continual weeping, she was back with us in Berlin, her plans for self-improvement in ruins.

She lost some of her spark after that. Her ebullient curiosity gave way to an indifference that might have been merely protective at first, but eventually seemed to enter the actual pigment of her personality. She stopped reading, and spent her evenings watching West German soap operas on the TV instead. Her eyes began to look a little sunken in their sockets. My mother got her a clerical job at the *Demokratischer Frauenbund Deutschlands* – the women's organisation where my mother herself now held an advisory position. She cleaned our apartment assiduously every morning before work, and every weekend drank herself to sleep in her little bedroom.

This was a period in which our whole household seemed to be in decline. As predicted, my mother had revived her soirées, on cue to garner the maximum admiration for her pluck without risking disapproval for an unseemly lack of grief over her misfortune. Uncle Heinrich still came, so most of the former habitués still thought it worthwhile to put in an appearance. But there was little pretence, now, of it being anything other than an act of calculated sycophancy. The atmosphere was that of a morgue – a morgue presided over by the king and queen of the underworld, in the shape of Heinrich in his dapper suit, gold party pin in his lapel, and my mother in her ice-blotched crown. I learned somewhere that the Japanese language used to have a particular verb form, the 'play form', reserved for addressing the nobility. Decorum required one to suppose that everything these privileged beings did was motivated by pleasure alone. Instead of saying, *You're building a new palace*, one would say, *You* play *building a new palace*. It seems to me that life at home during this period was qualified by a similarly attenuating form: not the play form but the *posthumous* form. *Posthumously*, people stood about at our soirées making glacial conversation. They nibbled posthumously on little underworld nuggets served by Kitty, who drifted posthumously among them like a pallid wraith. To the relief, no doubt, of everybody, no mention was made of my poetry, though I might well have posthumously gone through that rigmarole again if anyone had suggested it, so passive had I become.

The lines of force that had once seemed to plunge from the very source of meaning directly into our lives, shaping and patterning everything we did, had somehow been torn from us. We were unmoored. Events of a freakish, arbitrary nature had begun to occur, though in our posthumous condition we barely even registered their oddness. My father, for instance, began reappearing in the apartment, turning up unannounced, and staying for longer and longer intervals. My mother neither welcomed nor objected to his presence. She tolerated it, sometimes sitting with him in the living room as he silently reclined in his old armchair, sometimes ignoring him. He never stayed the night, and he avoided the soirées, but he was a fixture again, and though nothing was ever said, it was soon evident that he and my mother had re-established their marriage on a posthumous basis, him diminished beyond his already enfeebled stature, her in a position of unassailable yet entirely futile dominance.

Meanwhile, posthumously, my mother and I maintained the fiction that I was the family poet-intellectual. I stayed on at school past tenth grade to prepare for my *Abitur*. Posthumously, I sat through my classes, did my homework and took the exam. I was in bed with terrible flu when the results arrived. Through the bleary glaze of my fever I was aware of a subdued commotion in the apartment. I realised my mother was frantically making phone calls. Snatches of her conversation drifted into my throbbing head: *do something for Stefan? . . . too sensitive to perform well under that kind of pressure . . .* Gradually I understood that I had done poorly. In a dim, remote way, I felt my mother's anguish – another humiliation for our friends to enjoy – but I myself was indifferent. I burrowed back down into my fever, luxuriating in the oblivion, wishing it could last for ever. By the time I emerged from it, my mother, true to form, had warded off the calamity by sheer force of will, securing me a place to study philosophy at Humboldt University.

I had never shown the slightest interest in philosophy, but the subject was undersubscribed at that time, owing to a crackdown in the department. The notorious Professor Havemann had been ousted for introducing heretical texts into the syllabus, and a forbidding Marxist-Leninist orthodoxy now prevailed, putting off all but the most dedicated or desperate young men and women. In this way my mother found herself permitted to mention, casually, whenever the opportunity arose, her son 'the philosophy student, yes, at Humboldt.'

But Kitty.

One summer my mother took us off for a vacation on the island of Rügen. It was just the three of us: herself, me and Kitty. Otto had decided to pursue a career in the military – another turn of events that at one time would have stunned us; would have had to be discussed, analysed, cocooned in acceptable phrases, until it could be honourably accommodated into the grain of our identity as a family, but which we now, in our benumbed, posthumous fashion, accepted with a shrug as part of the general unexpectedness of things – and he was away on manoeuvres.

The weather was good. The Baltic waves seemed to relax from their solemn and exclusive duty as the concealers of Soviet submarines, and emitted an occasional gratuitous sparkle.

We stayed in a concrete beach hut rented out by a state hotel in Kühlungsborn. It was peaceful enough that we could each settle into our own rhythms, and a characteristically posthumous, atomised little holiday seemed set to ensue. My mother had taken up oil painting, and spent the days on a sand dune painting seascapes. Kitty lay on the beach listening to the radio and sunning herself. I stayed in the little house most of the time, smoking cigarettes in luxurious defiance of Dr Serkin's orders, and reading about Joseph Stalin. As a student at Humboldt I had access to books that were otherwise unavailable, including a large trove of both pre- and post-1956 (the year Khrushchev denounced him) tomes on the illustrious tyrant, in whom I had developed perhaps the only genuine intellectual interest I have ever known. I was reading about the years before the revolution, when his personality was just beginning to declare itself. In 1913 he was exiled to a remote region of Arctic Siberia. The temperature fell to minus forty in the winter, and swarms of mosquitoes made life almost as unbearable in the summer. An occasional care package arrived from the Alliluyev family in the Caucasus. Once, in a letter thanking them, Stalin asked for postcards with scenes of nature on them. 'I have a stupid longing to look at some landscape,' he wrote, 'if only on a piece of paper.' I was struck by the unexpectedly plangent tone of this. That this 'grey and colourless mediocrity', as Trotsky called him, could have possessed anything so poetic as a capacity for yearning; that the man in whom, later, a casual whim of displeasure could result in fifty thousand political prisoners in Bamlag being wired together like logs, trucked into the wilderness and shot, could ever have experienced feelings of longing for the natural world, was fascinating to me. I was lying on my bed reflecting on it – not in an analytic spirit so much as an aesthetic one – idly revolving it as one might a scene one has been unexpectedly struck by in a film or novel, when Kitty came into the room in her swimsuit.

My room led to the shower, and that appeared to be where she was heading. But before she got to the bathroom door, she came to a halt, slowed involuntarily, it seemed, by some thickness in the air. She stood rather vacantly for a moment, then peered at me.

'It's dark in here.'

I could tell from her voice that she was in an odd mood. It was early for her to be returning from the beach, and I wondered if she had had too much sun. She blinked in a bewildered, sunstruck way. I could smell the sea on her, and the oily sweetness of her tanning lotion. Her cheeks were a hectic crimson. She smiled distractedly, then moved on towards the bathroom. As she opened the door, she turned back.

'Where's your mother?'

Again something quizzical and involuntary in her stance, as though she had been struck like a bell, and these words were what chimed out. *Where's your mother?*

I shrugged. 'Out.'

As I said this, my eye met hers and something unexpected and momentous travelled between us.

I barely noticed Kitty in those days. She was just a part of the neutral human furniture of my life, as I assume I was of hers. It was a shock, then, to find myself staring into the grey depths of her eyes, which stared back in a manner both startled and intrepid, as if daring me not to look away and pretend that what had just happened had not. And as though some barrier between us had just been removed, I was suddenly physically aware of her as a woman.

It was she who broke off the look, moving on into the bathroom to take her shower. I returned to my book. It didn't reveal whether the Alliluyevs ever sent Stalin the postcards he asked for. I knew that he later married the daughter, Nadezhda, and that after they quarrelled at a party in the Kremlin, she went home and killed herself, though rapidly, as the effect of Kitty's look kept expanding inside me, all of this started to seem quite far away, and I found myself in a strange state comprised equally of arousal and anxiety. It occurred to me that Kitty's innocent question about my mother must have touched on some latent veto lodged in each of us, setting it flashing like an alarm light, and that it was this that had given our look its peculiar intensity. I saw her eyes again – the transparent grey like heat shadows on a wall – and a great jolt of desire went through me. I tried to read on about Stalin. Even in that godforsaken place, he chose to cultivate aloofness rather than sociability, pressing his granite-like ego against the fellow Bolshevik who shared his hut, till the man moved out. I remembered how Otto had once admitted to me that he fantasised about Kitty when he jerked off. He was always very frank about sex; said he liked to imagine doing it to her from behind, one hand over each of her breasts. The image of him sneaking up on the 'upward-aspiring' Kurt Teske bronze in our living room and groping her billowy breasts came back to me on a strange, rippling current of hilarity. I exchanged the Kurt Teske for Kitty in my mind's eye, then Otto for myself, half consciously donning his free and easy personality over mine – a psychic mask. At once I felt startlingly alive; full of odd, crackling powers. Kitty came out of the shower wrapped in a towel, her darkened, steel-coloured hair straggling over her cheeks. I looked at her with a brazenness that stalled her and seemed to confuse her for a moment. Then, to my amazement, she giggled and ran out of the room. Without thinking, I got up and went after her. She ran into the dining room, looking back at me with bursts of high, breathless laughter, and before I knew it I was chasing her around the furniture like some priapic satyr pursuing a scantily clad nymph, until I caught her and we fell together on the sticky plastic of the living room sofa. As I held her there, my hands on the soft muscles of her arms, she looked up at me with an expression of calm and – to my eye – somewhat sceptical curiosity, as if to say, *So? And now what are you proposing to do?* I was more or less inexperienced in these matters. I had exempted myself from the sexual fray at Humboldt, in the belief that, damaged as I was, entering it would only result in pain and humiliation. Now, as Kitty looked at me, I could feel a multitude of blurry uncertainties beginning to teem. I found myself picturing Otto in the raindrop camouflage of his NVA *Felddienstuniform* and thinking of how I had been rejected from military service because of my TB, and had served instead with the Construction Brigade – the *Bausoldaten* – clearing woodland for army barracks, in the plain grey uniform of the noncombatant, my ignominious little shovel-insignia gleaming at my shoulder. For an anxious moment these images threatened to pry away the Otto-self with which I had armoured my own, but then – such was my peculiar cast of mind at that time – I was fortified by the sudden, reassuring memory that Stalin too had been turned down for military service, because of a childhood injury to his left arm, and with a feeling of cold, brutal lust, I tore the towel off Kitty and began ineptly mauling her naked body. She lay observing me dispassionately for a few moments, then sat up, putting her hands over mine with soft firmness.

'No, Stefan,' she said without rancour. 'Not like that. Here . . .'

She put her hands on either side of my head and, gently bringing my lips to hers, began pouring her soft, wounded, passionate being into mine with a tenderness so entirely novel to me it was a source almost as much of bewilderment as of pleasure. Still kissing me, she placed my hands on her breasts, which were considerably softer than those of Kurt Teske's bronze nude, a fact that didn't exactly surprise me, but clashed distantly against some unconscious preconception I must have held concerning the pliability of female breasts, and, murmuring, 'Gently, Stefan; gently, gently,' proceeded to initiate me into her own peculiarly sweet-natured brand of love.

An unaccustomed warmth filled me in the aftermath. When my mother came home, I smiled at her affectionately, and found myself lavishing praises on the new canvas she was carrying. She glanced at me, a brief wariness stirring in her eyes, but seeing that I was sincere, she softened, growing almost bashful.

'Oh, it's just a mess, don't you think?'

'Not at all, it's gorgeous. They all are.'

'Really? Do you mean that, Stefan?'

A feeling of tenderness brimmed in me – it had been years since I had glimpsed this childlike, vulnerable creature she guarded under her formidable exterior.

'I do.'

'You don't think they're horribly amateurish?'

'I think they're wonderful.'

I looked from her to the paintings leaning against the living room wall – a series of semi-abstract seascapes, each one favouring a different shade of blue.

'Hmm. Well, perhaps I'll donate one or two of them to the local DFD,' she said. 'These branch offices never have anything interesting on the walls. Or perhaps I should just burn them. What do you think, Kitty?'

'No, don't burn them,' Kitty said with a dutiful look of alarm.

'You think they're worth holding on to?'

'Yes! They're pretty.'

'Pretty!' my mother scoffed. 'Well, if that's all they are, I certainly *shall* burn them.'

'Oh, no! I didn't mean – I just – I don't know anything about art . . .'

This brought a more forgiving look from my mother. 'Ah, but there's nothing you need to know,' she said, 'all you need is to be able to look with your *eyes* and *feel*. Look at this one here. I've tried to make the ocean express a sort of mood – do you see? Something a little sombre, even sad.'

'Oh, yes. It *is* sad! It's very sad –'

'Sad but –'

'I feel sad just looking at it now.'

'Ah, but wait,' my mother said patiently, 'it's not as simple as that. Look up in this corner, here. See?'

'These blobs of yellow?'

'Well, think of them as a tonality, relative to the rest; a modifier.'

Kitty looked lost. A bewildered, innocent expression settled on her.

'It's lighter here, isn't it?' my mother persisted. 'Lighter than the rest. Like a little, subtle suggestion of –'

'You mean a ray of hope!' Kitty exclaimed.

'Well, that's putting it more crudely than I would hope was the case, but yes.'

'A picture of sadness with a sort of gleam of hope. I *see* now. That's so beautiful. Isn't that beautiful, Stefan?'

I nodded, smiling rapturously at her. It was all I could do to stop myself from kissing her, right there in front of my mother.

As it turned out, she had enough wisdom, or instinct for self-preservation, to bring our affair to a firm end before we got back to Berlin. On our last night in Rügen I crept quietly into her room. Instead of letting me into her bed as she had the previous nights, she frowned.

'No, Stefan, no,' she whispered. 'This isn't sensible at all. Go back to your room.'

'What? Let me in!'

'Ssh! Your mother . . .'

'I'll make it creak even louder if you don't –'

With a look of reproach, she moved to the side of her narrow bed. I climbed in beside her, enveloping myself in the still-intoxicating stale sweetness of her sheets.

98

She wore a ruffled white nightgown. I started to kiss her cream-moistened face. She pulled away.

'What's the matter?' I whispered.

She switched on a reading light and thrust her face close to mine.

'Look at me, Stefan.'

'I'm looking.'

'I'm twelve years older than you. Look at these dark circles under my eyes. They don't go away, you know. Not any more. And these little furrows around my mouth. Soon they're going to start bunching up like there's a drawstring under them. Find someone your own age.'

I planted a kiss on the offending mouth, then slid my hand over her nightgown. She threw back the covers and yanked up the cotton shift, baring herself. Grabbing my hand, she squeezed it onto the flesh of her inner thigh.

'Feel how loose that is?' she hissed. 'It's about to start really sagging. Same with these.' She moved my hand to a gravity-shallowed breast. 'See? I'm like a piece of melting cheese. Is that what you want in a woman? I'm too old for you. *That's* what the matter is.'

She eyed me resentfully. I felt obscurely flattered. A sensation of manly protectiveness swelled inside me. I kissed her again; felt her take pleasure in it in spite of herself. Her fatigued, careworn prettiness touched me to the quick. The room, lit by her reading lamp, was neat and absolutely bare – herself its single ornament. I felt as though I were embracing a bouquet of fragile, frailly tinctured flowers. I could see nothing beyond my need to prove myself as a man capable of taking full possession of his woman. The more she resisted, the more imperative this need became. I ran my hand down over her waist.

'No, Stefan, really . . .'

'Why not?'

She sat up, covering herself again. 'You're practically my brother, Stefan. Doesn't that disturb you?'

'No.'

'Well, it should. This is – it's incest!'

She gave a little winsome laugh as she said this. I smiled, pulling her back down to the pillow and bringing her mouth to mine, emboldened by a thin, metallic confidence that had been steadily awakening in me since we first made love. She yielded a little: confused, warily responsive. I was beginning to understand the mechanisms within her that had set the patterns of her life; the little cogs and levers of self-doubt, kindness, irrational passion.

'Please, Stefan, please.'

'But why?'

Her pale cheeks were flushed, her eyes wild. 'I'm a vulnerable person. I'm very emotional. If we go on now, I'll get attached to you. That's the way I am.'

'So?'

'You don't want that.'

'I do, Kitty. That's exactly what I want.'

'Why? So you can feel how powerful you are when it comes time to move on to the next woman?'

'Kitty, don't be ridiculous . . .' However accurate the image of wrinkles and melting cheese she seemed intent on evoking may have been, this feeling of imminently triumphant possession was the more powerful reality, gilding her physical body with a layer of pure erotic substance that sent waves of desire through me at every touch. It was inconceivable to me that I might ever not want this.

'I don't want any other woman,' I said, surprising myself at how nobly sentimental the words made me feel.

But it was apparently these words that gave her the strength she was looking for. She drew away from me, gently but decisively, pulling her nightgown back down around her.

'Go to bed now, Stefan,' she said, smiling calmly at me. 'We'll be friends this way. Go on.'

And as effortlessly as she had set the current flowing between us, she made it stop. It was as though some very simple problem had been resolved. The desire sluiced out of me. Without further protest, with even a certain feeling of relief, I went back to my room. Neither of us ever alluded to the matter again.

But for some time afterwards, I was in an exalted state. That such intensities of joy as I had just experienced had all these years been lying in wait for me, hidden inside those days like a purse of gold lying on a traveller's path in some folktale, violently contradicted my sense of what life could possibly hold in store for me. It seemed after all that there was every reason to hope for happiness in this world.

CHAPTER 7

After I left Humboldt, I worked for a government organisation creating posters promoting 'Peace, Friendship and Anti-
Imperialist Solidarity'. The posters were put up in schools,
offices, hospitals and other public places. Sometimes they
solicited donations for Account 444, a public fund set up to
support developing countries, but their main intent was to
foster an image of the GDR as a beacon of conscience in a
cynical and dangerous world. Given the historic idealism of
my countrymen, who enjoy nothing better than the sensation of exclusive occupancy of the high ground in any landscape, moral or otherwise, this was not a difficult task. Even
the dissident types I was soon to meet approved of our
campaign. It takes a dubious sophistication to object to a
poster condemning apartheid, on the grounds that the body
condemning it isn't exactly a picture of health itself. At any
rate we didn't trouble ourselves with such scruples, and other
than the faint background suspicion that *everything* one could
do in that land was inherently tainted with futility and fraud-
ulence (our equivalent, perhaps, of the so-called 'hum of life',
the G-sharp that whines when all other noises stop), the work
was free of the more obvious kinds of stress.

Liaising between a state committee – the *Solidaritäts-
komitee der DDR* – and the Academy of Arts (whose president

was a close friend of Uncle Heinrich's), we commissioned and produced posters in support of the ANC, the Palestinians, the Laotians, the socialist opposition in Nicaragua, Chile and El Salvador and so forth. Our formula was simple: a compassion-arousing image of suffering in the third world, combined with an allusion to US imperialist culpability. A naively rendered Tree of Life, for instance, filled with delicate fruits in Sandinista colours, would stand with an air of tender pathos, about to be crushed by Uncle Sam's boot. A small African child would sit stoically, bound in huge chains embossed with the words 'US Steel'.

After a few months I was assigned to a group working on a series of purely anti-American posters – no pretext of *supporting* some other country. We showed the Statue of Liberty setting off a nuclear explosion with her torch; we had the stripes of the American flag rendered as the bars of a prison encompassing the entire planet. Anything we could think of that might stir up feelings of hatred for America was considered fair game. Hatred occupied a more reputable position in the spectrum of emotions back in the GDR than it does here in the States. I remember that among the sentiments chiselled on the walls of our assembly room at school were the words of Dr Lange, minister of education in the Soviet Zone after the war: 'Youth must be filled with hatred for the enemies of our peaceful constructive work.' There was nothing strange to any of us, therefore, about the idea of devoting ourselves to the arousal of this emotion in our compatriots. Our medium was the substance of righteousness itself. Handling it filled us with an almost luminous moral glow, like some benign form of radioactivity. I myself was no exception in this. I was entirely fulfilled in this job. I found I had a gift for propaganda – the triangulating of powerful images with latent phobias, to create a precisely targeted impulse of aggression – and I enjoyed exercising it. It also amused me to swap ideas with the skilful artists we summoned to our spruce-panelled offices on Lichtenberger-Strasse, and furthermore to find my suggestions being listened to with respect.

Best of all, the work brought me once again into a relationship with America. A treacherous relationship, of course, but as I have since found to be the case in so many circumstances, my private feelings of devotion not only survived within that outward form of hostility, but flourished. The more ingenious my contributions to our campaign of defamation, the more intense my feeling of secret connection to the US became. I have often wondered, in fact, whether betrayal and renunciation, far from negating people's attachments, might in fact be the means by which they make them indestructible.

IT WAS AT this time that I met Inge. At one of my mother's gatherings, a young composer named Walter Meyer was talking about new plays. He and his wife Clara, a television editor, were voracious consumers of contemporary culture, so abreast of the latest developments in all the arts that even my mother claimed to find them daunting. Walter mentioned a play by an avant-garde group that had just opened in Prenzlauer Berg.

'Clara and I were thinking of seeing it,' he said to me. 'Perhaps you'd like to come with us?'

I thanked him and said that I would. We arranged to meet the following weekend.

Prenzlauer Berg in those days was something like the East

Village was when Inge and I first arrived in New York: a mixture of the decrepit and the bohemian. Most of the workers' families who used to live there had moved out of the crumbling old Wilhelmine tenement houses to Marzahn or one of the other new satellite cities. In their place all sorts of misfits, outcasts and dubious artistic types (the kind my father had been afraid my mother might be introducing to our house all those years ago) had moved in, lacing the dark backyards and factory halls of the greenless quarter between Schönhauser and Prenzlauer Allee with a network of galleries, bars and performance spaces. I'd never spent much time there myself, but its vaguely disreputable aura had impressed itself on my imagination, and I set off to meet Walter and his wife that Friday evening with a feeling of adventurousness.

Walter and Clara were waiting for me outside the theatre, an old warehouse with tiny barred windows.

I was wearing a sports jacket and pressed pants from the Jumo department store. I remember becoming rapidly self-conscious about my over-formal appearance as we filed into the black-painted auditorium. Most of the other members of the audience were casually dressed, the men in faded jeans (real ones), the women in exotic, trinket-spangled garments I couldn't even name. Even Walter and Clara, though not exactly scruffy, knew enough to blend in.

With this petty but curiously upsetting matter on my mind, I found it hard to pay attention to what was happening onstage, at least until the main actress appeared. And when she did, far from making me concentrate on the play itself, the effect she had was simply one of bewilderment; bewilderment tinged with outrage. *Here's something else you'll never be able to have*, was the idea her presence aroused in me.

Undemonstrative to the point of seeming almost drugged,

she gave an appearance of immense, stilled, almost angry concentration, like some powerful and potentially dangerous machine. Physically she seemed imposingly tall and very slender (in reality she turned out to be of average height and weight). Her deep-set, blond-lashed eyes, high cheekbones, and excessively pale skin gave her a wraith-like look, further abetted by the blades of utterly straight white-blond hair falling either side of her face, and the curt slash of fringe across her forehead.

The interval came and I turned to Walter, intending to make some complimentary remark about the production and thank him for bringing me, when he said tersely:

'Let's get out of here, shall we?'

I gaped at him, startled.

'I mean, it's banal beyond words, no?'

Afraid of seeming naive, I converted my gape into a little indulgent grin, as if to say, *But of course, that goes without saying*.

'Come on, then. We'll get a drink somewhere instead.'

I followed him and Clara out. They seemed in a strange hurry to get away from the place.

That night, the image of the actress appeared in my mind with startling vividness. It was there when I woke in the morning too: a gleaming intrusion. And all day at work, it hovered like the persistent afterglow of a too-bright light over everything I said and did.

I would say the word for what I felt at that point was 'fascination', rather than 'infatuation'. She was out of my orbit – I was well aware of that; as remote from me as a distant star, and about as likely to be capable of returning my interest.

Nevertheless, I found myself going back to the theatre a few days later, alone.

This time I got the outfit right – a lumpy old coat that had belonged to my father, over a white T-shirt I'd bought from a Polish street vendor and then carefully stained with ink. I also tried to pay a little more attention to the play itself. It was called *Macbrecht*, and it was a weird mixture of satire, horror and surreal farce, about an ambitious playwright whose even more ambitious wife eggs him on to murder all his rivals until no plays but his own can be put on anywhere in the land. It was full of witches, phantom knives, blood-spattered ghosts and strange, mad incantations. Most of the jokes went over my head. I missed the allusion to William Shakespeare's *Macbeth*, didn't know enough about what I later heard described as 'Brecht Fatigue' to understand why our national cultural icon was being caricatured as a crazed megalomaniac, and was far too politically unaware to realise that the real object of satire wasn't Brecht at all, but the state that had enshrined him and decreed from on high all the other elements of our spiritual and political diet. All this I picked up later: at the time I was soon content to let it wash over me again, while I devoted my attention to the actress: Inge Leibus.

Again that double sense of an opening and a closing: of being given a glimpse of some new galaxy of sensations, and of simultaneously understanding that they could never be mine to experience. Anguish, then, though masked in the immediate moment by the simple rapture of beholding this otherworldly woman casting her lunar radiance over the obscure goings-on around her.

She didn't 'act' in any sense I was accustomed to: throwing away her lines, and making no attempt to match the nimble comic gestures of the other actors. No apparent effort of 'impersonation' to persuade one of the reality of the macabre creature she was playing; and yet that creature was conjured very palpably into existence.

I was aware that in addition to that quality of remoteness, her allure for me had something to do with the suggestion of a violently destructive power at her disposal. Hearing her calling on the spirits to fill her with cruelty, I was taken back to the time of my adolescence, when I used to fantasise about a force powerful enough to obliterate the entire universe, or at least the part of it I myself had been born into. It seemed to me that just such a force was contained within the tall, palely incandescent frame of this woman.

To the small extent that I was able to follow the plot, I understood that a coalition of victims' relatives and sympathisers was gradually forming against the murderous couple. In contrast to the Macbrechts' stiffly formal costumes, the actors playing these parts were dressed like the audience, in jeans and tattered jackets, with the odd flourish of punk ornamentation – dyed bristles, silver chains – such as one had begun to see occasionally in TV footage of street demonstrations and rock concerts.

At the climax of the play they converged on the theatre (now fortified) where the Macbrechts were holed up, some of them carrying leafy branches, like banners of a battalion from the Green Movement. Just as this motley army was about to defeat Macbrecht and his cohorts, there was a sudden commotion in the real theatre. Several men in dark clothing ran onto the stage from the auditorium. In a swift, violent convergence, they grabbed hold of certain of the actors and began yanking them off the stage by their hair and clothes, twisting their arms behind their backs and roughly dragging them down the aisles towards the exit.

For a moment I thought this was part of the play, and was

tremendously excited by the unexpected sense of mayhem it unleashed into the air. But even when I realised this wasn't the case, I didn't fully grasp what was going on until someone beside me pointed at the actors who were just then being frog-marched right past us, and said, '*Schwerter zu Pflugscharen*', and I saw for the first time that each of these actors was wearing a badge with the swords-to-ploughshares insignia on it.

This insignia, depicting a blacksmith hammering a large sword into a ploughshare, was the emblem of the unofficial peace movement. It had recently been outlawed as part of a crackdown on unsanctioned anti-nuclear activity, and you could get arrested for wearing it.

With their odd, almost squeamish punctiliousness, the authorities appeared to have decided to restrict their actions against the play to clear violations of the law, singling out only those actors sporting the offending emblem, and studiously ignoring everyone else.

It was all over very quickly, and there was something haughtily impartial about it, as though one had been witnessing a natural, nonhuman phenomenon. From outside we heard the slam of car doors and the roar of engines as the prisoners were driven off.

I could hear my mother's voice very clearly in my head, advising me to leave at once or risk 'receiving disadvantage'. I realised that Walter and Clara must have spotted the badges early on in the play the other evening and smelled trouble. That, rather than some lofty aesthetic scruple, had been the cause of their hasty departure. Not that I thought any the worse of them for having left: I probably would have scuttled off myself now if some absurd, entirely unwarranted sense of opportunity hadn't proved even stronger than my natural caution, and compelled me to linger.

The reaction in the theatre, after the first shock, was oddly muted. Some people did scuttle off. Others stood whispering in small groups, sneaking nervous looks around them. But still others seemed completely blasé, acting as if nothing at all unusual or significant had taken place.

Some of these now wandered onto the stage, where they stood smoking and talking with the remaining members of the cast. A tall, intelligent-looking young man in silver-framed glasses was chatting with the actor who had played Macbrecht, exchanging what I took to be wryly amusing comments about what had just occurred. After a moment, they were joined by the actress, Inge Leibus, still in costume.

I watched them standing there together in the glare of the stage lights. Something in their gestures, their facial expressions, their laconic, almost disdainful way of carrying themselves caused a wave of envious longing to travel through me. I stared at them from the relative darkness of my seat, mesmerised.

The auditorium was emptying out. Reluctantly, I made my way to the exit.

A woman with a bush of wiry curls came out of the theatre after me.

'Menzer's place,' she said to a group of people dawdling outside. At once they grew more animated. One of them called out to another group that had gone on ahead towards Kollwitzplatz:

'Hey – Menzer's place!'

The group turned back towards the theatre, picking up stragglers on the way, and then all of them began to move off. I stood there, wishing that I too could be a part of this cheerful expedition, but too shy, too close still to the days of my contagious unpopularity, to dare risking a snub by inviting myself along. Rain was falling, sour on the tongue and eyelids. I was about to cross the street to the U-Bahn when the curly-haired woman turned back to me. She gave me a brisk once-over, appraising me from top to toe. To my great joy, she appeared to judge me acceptable.

'Coming?' she asked, almost impatiently.

'Well, I – I haven't been invited.'

She tossed her head with a little scornful grimace. 'Don't have to be invited. It's open house at Menzer's. Everyone's welcome.'

I joined her.

'Margarete,' she said, shaking my hand as we set off together down the wet sidewalk of Saarbrücker Strasse.

'Stefan Vogel.'

She had a small face with thick brown eyebrows and a sharp red nose like a bird's beak.

'Poet?' she asked.

I looked at her, caught off my guard by this inaccurate but curiously pertinent guess. I found that I didn't want to deny it, though I couldn't quite bring myself to affirm it either.

'You don't look like a painter,' she added, as if by way of explaining herself.

'No –'

'Wrists too thin.'

'I'm not a painter.'

'What I thought.' She nodded, causing her chin to disappear for a moment into her plump neck.

I was aware of having somehow used an honest answer to establish false credentials.

'What about you?' I asked.

She gave a squeaky laugh. 'I'm nobody. I'm Margarete. Menzer's sister.'

We turned down an alley of derelict buildings with jet-black oblongs where the windows had been. At the end was a free-standing tenement house in better repair (the ground-floor windows were glazed, and the stucco walls appeared to have been spared the defective latex paint that had been slathered over just about everything in the seventies, only to flake off five years later, along with the stucco beneath). The front door was fastened with a heavy padlock. We stopped here, and stood waiting in the drizzle.

After a few minutes, the tall, bespectacled man I'd seen on the stage before came sauntering down the alley with his own entourage, among them the Macbrecht actor and Inge.

Smiling faintly at the rest of us while continuing his conversation, the man climbed the steps to the front door and unfastened the padlock.

My officious companion tapped me on the arm. 'That's Menzer,' she informed me with a little satisfied pursing of her lips. We followed this illustrious-looking personage into the house.

And so, in that casual manner, I entered into a new phase of my life: the last one before I left with Inge for the West.

CHAPTER 8

I say 'casual', and that was how it felt, but of course the more one learns about that place and those times, the less plausible the word 'casual' comes to seem in connection with even the most trivial aspects of one's life. From the vantage of the present it seems to me that even at this early stage in the drama that followed, the likelihood is that I was already under the interested scrutiny of powers outside myself, and was already submitting to the guidance of their first, imperceptibly gentle touches.

Inside Menzer's house, a bare-floored hallway led into a long, narrow room, cluttered with books, papers, paintings and odd bits of sculpture that on closer inspection turned out to be pieces of furniture improvised out of junk.

As the twenty or so of us trooped in, Menzer wandered across to a table where something appeared to have caught his eye. He picked up a piece of paper and glanced briefly over it. A look of remote amusement appeared on one side of his handsome face.

'What is it, Menzer?' a blond-bearded man asked eagerly. This man looked familiar to me, though I couldn't place him.

Menzer held out the piece of paper by a corner, though before the man could take it, Margarete darted forward and snatched it with a squeak of laughter. She scanned it rapidly.

'Menzer's got another Notice to Appear!' she exclaimed, handing the paper to the other man, who looked at it admiringly, then sent it circulating around the room. It passed through my own hands, though only long enough for me to take in the words *Notice to Appear* and *Normanenstrasse*.

'Why don't they leave you alone, Menzer?' a green-eyed young girl – no more than twenty – asked.

Menzer gave a barely perceptible shrug. 'Probably they just want to show me they can still get in the house without smashing down the door.' He crinkled one side of his mouth. 'It's almost funny.'

'But what will they do to you?'

'They'll keep me waiting in a cell for a few hours, then ask me what Westerners I've been in contact with. I'll say Ronald Reagan and the Pope. They'll threaten to close down the magazine. I'll tell them be my guest. Then with luck they'll give me back my Captain Beefheart albums which they stole last time around, and send me over the Wall in a private chopper.'

Everyone laughed. Bottles of Pilsator beer were opened, cigarettes lit, and some fast, loud music came bursting from a record player in the corner.

I sat on a painted wooden crate by a bookshelf, amazed to find myself here, and aware that the multitude of at once urgent-seeming and completely puzzling impressions I was absorbing would take time to understand. Aside from the laconically domineering presence of this man Menzer, the principal fact for me at that moment was that Inge Leibus was here in the same room as I was. For some time, out of a mixture of shyness and pride, I avoided looking at her, and spent several minutes studying the bookshelf beside me. On it was a row of books by what appeared to be French authors.

114

The books bore the imprint of a West German publisher, which in my eyes was in itself enough to confer on them an aura of something more like necromancy than literature.

'Who's out there?' Menzer called from across the room. He was addressing Macbrecht, who was standing near me, by the window. 'Yours or mine?'

Macbrecht looked down onto the alley.

'Yours – I think.'

Menzer ambled over to the window. A crumpled jacket hung from his narrow shoulders, and the flow of bulges and creases in the material was continued above it in his long, narrow, pale grey face, which owed its handsome effect less to any classical perfection of features than to an alluring but not quite decipherable play of asymmetries about the eyes and mouth, and some oddly placed muscular bumps and hollows down the cheeks, as though the whole form had been elongated and subtly misshapen, by stress perhaps, or unnatural use.

He opened the window.

'Werner,' he drawled, not bothering to raise his voice, 'come in, you idiot. It's too wet for you out there. You'll catch another cold.'

A moment later a sheepish-looking man with a wet moustache came through the door.

'Sit down, have a drink,' Menzer told him. Margarete darted off for a beer and gave it to the man, who looked at it uncertainly.

'Go on, man!' Menzer said, hoisting a friendly sneer from one side of his mouth. 'You think we'd waste our narcotics on the Firm?'

The man assumed a pious air. 'I don't acknowledge that I'm with the Ministry of State Security. I don't deny it, but I don't admit it either.'

This was greeted with jeering and laughter, not entirely hostile.

Macbrecht lumbered over – a pink-jowled, heavy-breathing man. He planted himself squarely in front of the new arrival.

'So what was that about, Werner, at the theatre?'

'What?'

'Are we going to get our actors back?'

'Oh, that.'

'Yes, that. Are we?'

The man shrugged, wiping his raggy moustache. He looked unhappily at the floor.

'That's Werner, with the moustache.' Margarete had reappeared at my side. 'Menzer's tail.' She nodded importantly.

'You mean Stasi?' I whispered. I was utterly bewildered.

Margarete made a harsh tutting sound. 'No need to whisper. It's open house here, I told you. Everyone's invited, Firm included. We're artists, not politicos. We don't want to reform the system. We're just completely bored by it, and we're too cynical to believe in trying to change it.'

Perhaps it wasn't quite so absurdly rote-like, what she actually said, but the way she said it made it sound like some kind of official statement of position.

Even so, the words themselves struck a chord in me. Boredom, cynicism . . . I could relate to that . . .

'Did you bring some poems?' she asked me.

'Well, no . . .'

'I'll show you some of Menzer's. Wait.'

She flitted off again. I turned back to the other conversation. It had broadened now, and become a little heated, though amicably so. The disagreement was between the theatre people on one side, and Menzer with some like-minded friends on the other. The Stasi man sat between them, morosely sipping his beer, and trying to put in the odd word of his own.

Menzer was talking. 'So let me get it straight –'

He had a nasal, bored-sounding voice, this weary prince, though with a note of incipient hilarity in it as you came to know it better, as if he were continually delighting himself with the things he heard himself say.

'You put on your swords-to-ploughshares badges, you get arrested, then you pretend to be outraged because that was just part of a costume and the cops should have made a distinction between a real illegal display and a metaphorical illegal display, and you create a little disturbance, a little event, and somehow all this is supposed to help avert a nuclear holocaust – is that the idea?'

'Well –' Macbrecht huffed.

'Somehow this is going to persuade the Central Committee to throw down its weapons and abandon the Warsaw Pact –'

'Well, but –'

'Menzer's got a point,' the Stasi man said.

'You shut up,' Menzer told him. 'Seriously, Benno, you think wearing a badge –'

'Not in itself, obviously,' another of the actors began.

'Do you even know where that image comes from?'

The actors looked uncertainly at each other. I noticed Inge furrowing her brow.

'Do you?' Menzer repeated with a grin.

'You mean the swords-to –'

'To-ploughshares, yes. That naked muscular blacksmith of yours. You don't even know where your own emblem comes from? Oh, that's almost funny!' He gave a harsh, crowing laugh.

'I know where it comes from,' I heard myself call out.

Several pairs of eyes, showing various degrees of quizzical interest, were suddenly gazing at me from across the room. Among them Inge's.

'It comes from a Soviet sculpture,' I said, projecting as much appeasing humility into my tone as I could (the last thing I wanted to do was offend anybody).

'That's right, of course,' Inge said softly. I looked at her directly for the first time now. She had changed out of her costume into a pale dress with blue tights, the plainness of which, far from diminishing her glamour, seemed rather to have been raised by its wearer to the same level of high expressiveness as the stylised robe she'd been wearing before, though this time in the service of simplicity rather than queenliness.

She smiled gratefully at me, and a surge of pleasure went through me.

'So even our protest symbols come down to us from the forces we're protesting against,' she continued. 'Is that your point?'

As on the stage earlier, her quiet voice commanded one's ear effortlessly, without the need of being raised, as though simply parting the sea of noise on either side of itself.

Menzer was unfazed: 'Yes, and I'm glad I don't have to spell it out, since that would be almost boring.'

'So what are *you* proposing?' the other actor asked.

'Nothing,' Menzer said with a smile. 'There's nothing you can do. Explore different kinds of silence. Otherwise absolutely nothing. You know as well as I do the whole language is occupied territory – has been for decades. Every time you say a word like *peace*, all you're doing is taking your tongue for a swim in a sea of shit.'

'Then why do you bother with your magazines? Why not just join the party and have a career like everyone else?'

118

Menzer shrugged. 'It amuses us to fuck with words. Doesn't it, Paul?' He turned to the familiar-looking blond-bearded man who had been standing by his side nodding at his remarks. I remembered suddenly where I had seen him before: in Wandlitz, disappearing off to play with Otto, while I stayed with his sister Katje. He was Katje Boeden's brother Paul.

'Yeah. Maybe if we fuck with them enough, they'll turn into something interesting.'

'Like an exit visa?' Inge said, addressing her words to Menzer, but glancing again in my direction, as if in appreciative acknowledgement of an ally.

'That would be fine by me,' Menzer replied.

Inge smiled at him, saying nothing. The peculiar latent power I'd sensed humming inside her when she was onstage was still discernible, but I was struck now by the fact that it no longer felt violent or negative – quite the reverse, in fact: as herself, her strength seemed all gentleness. Her face looked softer – less sharply accentuated at the cheekbones, her hair less blindingly white, less severe in the lines it made against her cheeks and forehead. Only a slight burning quality about her eyes remained of the fanatic look she'd had before, and it seemed an entirely benign fanaticism now.

'Pretty, isn't she?' came a voice to my side. Margarete had returned.

I must have frowned involuntarily.

'It's OK, I already saw you looking at her in the theatre.' She grinned mischievously.

'Fiancé's in Jena. Ignoring her as usual. Hasn't even been to her play. Here, Menzer's poems –'

She handed me a small pamphlet with a nonsensical title made out of numbers and punctuation marks. There was a signed etching of a paper clip on the cover.

I opened it and looked at some of the poems. Though these were made out of real words, they too seemed to me nonsensical, partly no doubt because I was still absorbing the news that Inge had a fiancé, and trying to conceal the absurdly inappropriate dismay this had provoked in me.

CHAPTER 9

'Inge Leibus was asking who you were after you left the other night,' Margarete said to me a few days later in the Mikado Café off Kollwitzplatz. Before I had left Menzer's place Margarete had made a point of telling me I would be welcome at other such impromptu gatherings, giving me the addresses of various locations where they were likely to take place.

'Really? What did you tell her?'

'I told her you were a poet. A great admirer of hers – her acting, I mean.'

She smirked at me, sheathing her sharp little chin in its cushion of neck flesh. I assumed that her telling me all this was purely tactical: showing herself to be my ally in my pursuit of Inge, so that she could be my consoler when that pursuit failed. Women of her kind of borderline ugliness (to be blunt about it) had gone after me even at Humboldt, evidently considering me to be within their range.

A day or two later she brought me to an apartment not far from Menzer's where something between a party and a colloquium was taking place, with people packed into a spartan, smoke-filled room, talking heatedly about the imminent destruction of the planet.

Inge was there; again dressed simply, but costumed in her own pale beauty that set her in another plane of being – so it seemed to me – from the lesser mortals congregated in the room.

Margarete insisted on taking me over to meet her properly. She was listening to an agitated old man with thick-lensed glasses and purple, spittle-flecked lips. He was lecturing her on some peace-related matter, and words like '*Friedenssicherung*' and '*Friedenswerkstätten*' came sizzling out of his mouth in an angry effluvium of white foam.

Inge noticed me as Margarete and I drew near, and from a brief stilling of her blond-lashed eyes on mine (as pleasurable as being settled on by some beautiful blue and white butterfly), she seemed pleased to see me. But the old man kept haranguing her, and she either couldn't or wouldn't initiate the process of polite disengagement that convention allows at such moments.

I watched her listening to him: nodding respectfully, almost meekly, as he laboured through his points (an old-time utopian socialist, it appeared, he was cranking out some line about the inherent pacifism of orthodox Marxism); too sweet-natured to manoeuvre herself out of range of his saliva, or rather (as I came to understand) too conscientiously preoccupied with matching his urgent communicativeness with an answering attentiveness of her own, to notice.

This attentiveness was one of the qualities I came to love most deeply about Inge; this helpless, profligate giving of herself to whatever creature, human or otherwise, came before her with its needs and demands. In practical terms it could be exasperating – the world's most crashing bores and self-pitying narcissists, who have an unerring instinct for this kind of natural listener, tended to converge on her wherever she went, and I often had to resort to quite brutal means of dragging her away. But when I picture her now I always see her in this attentive state: her slender body tilting, slightly attenuated, towards the other person, her head at a quizzical angle in its straight-hanging arch of silken hair, her lips which seemed to have a little extra upturning red length at the corners (as if for the expression of joys beyond the capacity of normal humans to experience) open in a gentle smile, her serious eyes proffered like pools of grey-blue, restorative waters.

The old man certainly wasn't about to give her up without a fight. When Margarete finally put her hand on Inge's arm to interrupt her, he just went on talking, only louder and faster, as if his life depended on it, glaring at me furiously. I started to back away, but Inge, aware now of the possibility of wounding someone else's feelings in addition to his, made a confused attempt to acknowledge Margarete and myself, while still listening to him. I dwell on these minutiae in order to give a sense of what I perceived about Inge at that moment: that she was possessed of an extreme, perhaps even overdeveloped human feeling, and that she was someone for whom the world was evidently too much at times: someone perhaps in need of protection.

When the old man finally shut up (standing his ground, though, with his lips ominously pursed as though waiting for the first opportunity to unleash another torrent), and Margarete introduced us, I said the first thing that came into my head, which was that I didn't want to take any of her time, but I just had to tell her how wonderful I thought her performance had been in *Macbrecht*. Instead of laughing off the compliment, as I expected her to do, she coloured deeply and gave me an awkward smile.

'Did you really think so?' she asked.

'Absolutely!' I assured her.

She seemed uncomfortable with the flattery, and yet when the old man seized her back and I moved politely away, I did so with the distinct feeling that she had been half hoping for me to continue in the same vein.

CHAPTER 10

Early evening. Fifteen or twenty people grouped around the chipped marble tables of the Mikado Café. I wandered in, taking a seat at the edge and nodding at my new acquaintances. Inge was there. She smiled at me, but distractedly, and before I even consciously registered who the person sitting next to her must be, I felt my spirits sinking.

He was a large man, tall and very broad, with a reddish complexion that gave his lightly pigmented eyes a hot quality. I sensed immediately that he was not one of my kindred spirits from the *privilegentsia*: a decade or two of physical labour was clearly visible in the knotted ligatures of his enormous hands, which sat restlessly before him on the round tabletop, crouched and alert-looking.

I didn't hear him speak much on that occasion, but he was unmistakably the centre of attention. The impact of a recent graffiti campaign in Weimar was being discussed, and most of the remarks were addressed directly to this man. He acknowledged each with a smile – brief, but managing to convey considerable warmth in its short moment.

He was from Jena, that much I knew. What Prenzlauer Berg was to Berlin, Jena was to our republic as a whole. Napoleon had smashed the Prussian army there. Marx received his doctorate from the university. The Workers' Uprising that nearly toppled Ulbricht and his cronies in '53 was sparked off in its streets. And now, thirty years later, it was a hotbed of what our security services labelled 'hostile-negative activity'. Doubtless I was projecting a certain envious admiration, but all this seemed contained in this man's fiery aura.

Inge looked tense beside him, I remember thinking; a bit diminished in his presence. She was hanging on his words, his silences rather, with her characteristic watchful attentiveness, though in a manner more suggestive of anxiety than the simple generous empathy it usually conveyed. The two of them left the café soon after I got there, followed by a man I took to be their tail (these things were conducted with blatant openness), and the gathering quickly lost its coherence.

'Thilo Hartman,' came the voice of Margarete, who had sidled up behind the gilt-bronze chair I'd perched myself on. 'Inge's fiancé. Turned up last night. They're in a big fight already.'

I nodded, having by now guessed who the man was. I didn't ask what the fight was about – I was feeling suddenly reluctant to acknowledge any interest in Inge, even to myself. Margarete told me the story anyway. Thilo had arrived in Berlin last night, but instead of going to see Inge in *Macbrecht* (the actors had been released, and the play was on again, without the badges), he had spent the evening with another friend, a woman.

'They have an open relationship,' Margarete informed me with a knowing look, 'both ways, though only Thilo takes advantage of it these days. He's always pushing her to go out with other men, but she won't – not any more. She claims not to care about the girlfriends. What makes her mad is he refuses to take her acting seriously. Won't even bother seeing her plays.'

126

'It doesn't sound as though they're too well suited to each other,' I said, affecting a yawn of indifference.

'He was just in prison,' she continued, ignoring my comment. 'Supposed to've been serving a three-year sentence, but they let him out . . .'

I listened to the story, unsure whether Margarete was trying to taunt me with the feebleness of my achievements next to those of my rival, or spur me into action, but either way I found myself feeling increasingly deflated as she spoke. He and some others had staged a silent protest in the main square in Jena, sitting in a circle and unfurling a banner with the word *Peace* on it. A so-called 'Working Class Combat Group' had beaten them up and dragged them off to jail, where they would have been languishing still, had there not been an international outcry on their behalf, prompting the authorities to free them. Most of the protesters had been expatriated – sold to the West for hard currency under the *Freikauf* system that Inge and I were eventually to take advantage of. But not Thilo:

'He wouldn't go. He refused!'

Unlike so many of his radical brethren, Thilo had apparently no desire to convert his oppositional temperament into a ticket out. His business, as he saw it, was here among the browbeaten souls of our republic – working men and women whose parched existences he was intimately familiar with from the large variety of jobs he'd held since leaving school at sixteen. Margarete listed these for me – glassblowing in the former Zeiss factories in Jena, shipping beets and barley in thousand-ton barges down the Saale River, hacking out lignite from the strip mines of northern Thuringia – her tone, whatever her intent, reaching me as distinctly taunting.

'They could have expelled him but they didn't want another

Biermann on their hands,' she concluded with a sadistic little smile. Wolf Biermann, poet and folk idol, whose forced expatriation a decade or so earlier had given the opposition an unforeseen rallying point. Hearing Thilo's name coupled with his was galling to me, to say the least.

'And meanwhile he can't be bothered to see his fiancée's plays,' I said, intending to strike a note of lofty, detached scepticism about the man's character.

'Ah, but they're in love,' Margarete replied.

As I looked for the usual glint of mischief in her eyes, I saw to my dismay that for once she was speaking in earnest.

And she was right: they were deeply in love, these two; and despite their difficulties, they were well suited too. In an exhibit of Aztec art that Inge and I saw a few years later in New York was a life-sized sculpture of a naked young man and woman sitting cross-legged next to each other, gazing fiercely out into the distance, each with a hand casually on the other's knee. The moment I set eyes on it I thought of Inge and her former fiancé. With their burning, outward-directed gazes, their affection – so casually signalled but nevertheless the attitude they were carrying forward into eternity – their vulnerable aura from having been immortalised in a condition of such fierce and youthful vitality, they called to mind the relationship I had insinuated myself into, bringing it back so powerfully and painfully that I almost blurted out loud: *That's you and Thilo* . . .

The 'open' nature of their relationship both was and was not as Margarete described it. It may have been true that in practice it applied more to Thilo than Inge, but it wasn't the opportunistically one-sided proposition I'd understood it to be from Margarete's description.

Inge revealed to me that the arrangement had been her

128

idea in the first place – an attempt (characteristically well intended and extreme) to accommodate the full, complicated reality of their needs and desires as adult human beings; a deliberate refusal to flinch from any truth about themselves simply because that might cause pain. And I learned from Thilo that his attempts to get Inge to 'spend time', as he put it, with other men was sincere to the point that he himself sought out men he thought she would get along with, and sent them in her direction, and furthermore that when she did decide to spend time with one or another of them, he, Thilo, would be racked by such torments of jealousy that on one occasion he had actually bitten a mouthful of flesh out of his own forearm to drown out the pain. He'd shrugged at my bewildered look (I was out of my depth in these waters): 'You love someone,' he said, 'so you want them to be free. And you want to be free yourself. Here, see . . .' He pulled up his shirtsleeve. The scar, a jagged-edged crater in the reddish-haired swale of muscle below his elbow, remains in my mind's eye as the counterpart to Brandt's livid disfigurement: it was the badge of a mad, fanatic, passionate innocence.

CHAPTER 11

'. . . Yes, but if one has devoured the language, then one has eaten the order it represents as well . . .'

Menzer again. Holding court amid the book piles and junk furniture of his spacious squat.

The occasion was a new issue of one of his literary magazines. He and his friends published several of these magazines, filling them with esoteric poems and articles.

'Where've you been? Inge's been asking for you,' Margarete had told me when I drifted back to Prenzl'berg (as I had now learned to call it) after a few days' absence. 'Come to Menzer's tomorrow. She'll be there – alone. Fiancé's back in Jena.'

And there she was, frailly luminous in the afternoon light, sitting by the far window. She smiled at me. The smile, like all her expressions, had a cleanness about it: the transparent registering of a simple motion of the heart, unclouded by the equivocations that afflict most of the looks one receives in adult company.

'Hello, Robert,' she said.

'Stefan,' I corrected her.

'Stefan! Of course! How stupid of me! I'm so sorry!' She looked so upset by her mistake that the sting it caused me gave way at once to a chivalric urge to protect her from her own mortification.

'Don't worry about it – please!'

She gestured at the seat beside her – a stool made of stacked tyre hubs – and I sat down. We looked at each other in silence for a moment, while Menzer's drawl rose over the din of other voices across the room, buoyed on its little cushion of self-delight.

'. . . a poetics of silence speaking between the signs . . . Absolute bankruptcy of the language of power . . .'

'How's the play going?' I asked Inge, my own voice sounding a little thin in my ear.

'It's finished. We're rehearsing a new one.'

'Oh, yes? What is it?'

She told me about the new play. She seemed to enjoy talking about it, and as I wanted her to associate me with pleasurable sensations, I questioned her at some length. In our last conversation I had formed the suspicion that she mightn't be altogether immune to flattery, and I found myself looking for opportunities to make subtly complimentary remarks about her acting. She responded to these with evident pleasure – not in a way that suggested any conceit about her work; quite the opposite: even though she had performed in several major productions, she turned out to be insecure about her abilities. She told me that she had never had any formal training.

'That's astonishing!' I heard myself exclaim. 'How did you learn to control an audience like that?'

'Oh, I don't . . . Well . . . It's nice of you to say that . . .'

'I mean it.'

She settled her eyes on mine, her expression neutral. I felt her taking my measure, sizing me up on some delicate internal instrument of appraisal; not yet entirely sure, after all, what it meant to be complimented by this newcomer to her circle.

131

After a while Menzer and his friends read poems from the new magazine. Paul Boeden, Katje's blond-bearded brother, read first, delivering his lines in what seemed to me an affected monotone. When Menzer himself followed, I saw where Paul had borrowed the tone from, though in Menzer's case the flatness seemed natural, even compelling; as though one were being read to by a dead man – a grey-skinned, shadow-filled ghost, come from beyond the grave to amuse himself with some private joke at the expense of the living.

Klaus Menzer, that supremely detached man . . . In the first of two interviews he gave *Stern* after reunification, I caught at once that amused, bored, circuitously self-aggrandising air of his. My mother had sent me the piece. 'Total indifference to the Stasi was our attitude.' I could hear the languid drawl. 'They'd drag me in for questioning every few months, but I never cared – didn't even hold it against them . . .' He got his artist's visa, his *Kunstlervisum*, in '87, a year after Inge and I had left, and set up in West Berlin as an art critic, his pronouncements on the death of this or that time-honoured medium of human creativity – sculpture, painting, drawing – rapidly establishing him as a player at the high-stakes museum-culture tables of Western Europe. His second interview, a year after the first, was another story altogether, and I must try not to let it colour my portrayal of the Menzer I knew, or thought I knew. The truth was I admired him – so much that I even began borrowing some of his mannerisms myself. *It's almost funny*, I would hear myself drawling, or *it's almost boring* . . . And even knowing what I do know about him now, I am hardly in a position to despise him. That, as he might say, would be *almost hypocritical*.

After the reading was over, I turned back to Inge, intending

132

to continue monopolising her. But before long Paul Boeden came up and stood just behind me.

'How's life, Inge?' he said, cutting right across me.

In her usual flustered way, Inge looked helplessly back and forth between us. With a show of good grace, I moved aside to make room for Paul. He gave me a brisk nod. Though we hadn't mentioned our shared past, I had the sense that he knew who I was, and this made me wary of him. He also appeared to be on easy terms with Inge, which further added to my discomfort at his intrusion.

I am trying to account here for the ill-judged step I made a few minutes after he joined us.

Inge had just congratulated him on his reading.

'Stefan's a poet too,' she said. 'Isn't that right, Stefan?' she added, putting her hand on my arm. 'Margarete told me . . .'

I knew she was saying this just to make conversation, but her gesture – the warm interest it seemed to promise if only what she was saying were in fact the case – made me momentarily giddy.

'A poet? Really?' Paul asked, raising an eyebrow. I felt suddenly that he knew exactly who I was – knew all about my father's disgrace, perhaps even about my own humiliation at the hands of his sister, and that in his mind this gave him the right to look down on me.

Among the few things I took in during my stint in the Philosophy Department at Humboldt was the idea – I forget whose – that the underlying motive for all human action is the desire for *recognition* – recognition of one's worth and dignity as a human being, without which one was a nonperson; a slave. The concept had articulated very precisely the obscure cravings of my own soul, and it had lodged itself in my imagination. It had felt incontrovertible. And it was

133

surely what motivated me now as I replied to Inge and Paul's question with a gesture of assent – half nod, half shrug – feeling instantly the immense weariness of spirit that, in my experience, accompanies the discharging of all such acts of self-destructive folly.

'Yes, that's right,' I said.

'Oh, yeah?' Paul replied, baring his teeth in a smile that seemed to me fully Brandtian in its mocking incredulity. 'Where can we read some of your stuff?'

I hesitated. Inge was looking at me with a pleasant, inno-cent smile, waiting politely for the simple answer to a simple question. I didn't feel that she herself was all that curious as to where she could read my 'stuff', and my answer, when I gave it, wasn't to impress her so much as to prevent any sugges-tion arising in her mind that I might be a less than straight-forward character. As far as Paul was concerned, I perhaps *was* guilty of wanting to impress him; to force him to 'recognise' me. The situation became further complicated by the fact that Menzer, who had been wandering in our direction, was now within earshot. With a feeling of reckless abandon, I blurted:

'*Sinn und Form.*'

'*Sinn und Form?* No kidding!'

Sinn und Form had been the leading journal of the literary establishment throughout my childhood, and as far as I knew, still was. My Uncle Heinrich was a subscriber and occasional contributor, and always brought the latest issue with him when he came to visit. I never read it, but its sober appear-ance, lying on the coffee table, was as permanent a feature in my private landscape as the Kurt Teske nude or the American radio (before Otto smashed it). It was a part of who I was, which is no doubt why its name tripped so readily off my tongue.

134

'Have I died of boredom or did I just hear the words *Sinn und Form*?' Menzer drawled, joining us.

'This man's published his poems there,' Paul told him.

Menzer looked at me, as if noticing me for the first time. To my surprise he treated me to a smile – a half smile, at least – and held out his hand to me.

'By the way, I'm Menzer,' he said. 'We haven't met properly.'

'Stefan Vogel.'

'I didn't mean to be rude there. That's good, getting your stuff in *Sinn und Form*. Almost impressive. I used to try them myself. They never accepted anything, so naturally I pretend to despise them for being hopelessly middle-of-the-road. Which issues are your poems in? I'd like to read them.'

I'd seen that last bit coming, at least, and by the time he got to it, my sprinter's imagination, with its knack for the short-term solution, had come up with an answer:

'They were only just accepted. I think they'll be out in the next issue.'

'Good. Well, be sure to bring it along when it comes out.'

'I will.'

'I'd like to read them too,' Inge said, smiling at me.

And there I was: back on the treadmill again, back in my little hell of vainglory, deceit, and desperate expedient. And whereas the price before had merely been a few years of my manhood, it was now apparently to be my soul.

CHAPTER 12

I see that I am slowing down as I reach this part of my story. As a matter of fact, I seem to be grinding to a halt. It's October now – almost a month since I began: a month-long torrent of memory, spilling out with unexpected swiftness and ease. (Possible I overestimated this writing business? It seems straightforward enough when you have something to say.) But now I feel as though I'm back in my room on Micklenstrasse before I raided my mother's trunk, trying to wring a poem out of my own dry brain . . . I seem to have a strong reluctance, even now, to resurrect the events that took place over the next few months: dusting off the old anthology to create another little set of masterpieces (Brandt had gone by then, replaced by an obliging woman with a cheerful smile for everyone); taking them up to my Uncle Heinrich in his book-filled room in the Office of the Chief of the People's Police; brazening out my own shame to ask if he would do me a little favour and recommend my efforts to the editors of *Sinn und Form* for their next issue . . .

Can't seem to drag myself back there. Can't bring myself to spell it all out even in the knowledge that I will be past caring by the time Inge or anybody else gets to read about it.

But speaking of that there is perhaps another factor in this sudden inhibition.

A few days ago I did something I'd been meaning to do for some time: double-check on the terms of our life insurance policy. Just as well I did, as I appear to have a certain amount still to learn about the defensive instincts of large capitalist institutions. It turns out that what I have in mind is not after all the ticket to an easy quarter of a million dollars for Inge. All the insurance company pays out in that event is the sum of what you've paid in: a few hundred bucks at most. So much for 'converting myself into gold'.

A blow. Not that the future awaiting me, so eloquently summarised by that glass of wine in my face, becomes any more conceivable. Life without Inge – a certainty once these revelations break her spell – is a prospect I have zero interest in pursuing. From my point of view she *is* life; all I want of life. I have felt this since I carried her off from Berlin, and the years since have merely strengthened that feeling. Even so, without the consoling lustre of making her rich (or at least giving her the means to relaunch herself into her own life), the act of aborting that future becomes suddenly a bleaker, starker matter. Hence, no doubt, my Scheherazade-like reluctance to get to the end of this tale.

Perhaps I should simply tell what happened from Inge's point of view; that way I could get around certain more delicate matters arising from my visit to my uncle, without being untruthful.

If I did this, the story would present Thilo's sudden rejection of Inge as an act of inexplicable callousness on his part, unwarranted even by the fact of his latest arrest, this time on the graver than usual charge of sedition.

Out of the blue (this version would go), hand-delivered by our ever-solicitous friend Margarete Menzer, Inge receives a smuggled jail note from her fiancé, telling her coldly to forget about him, advising her to forget about politics too and concentrate on her acting, since that was evidently where her heart was, and then laconically informing her that a few days before his arrest he had married an old girlfriend in Jena, a full-time activist in the peace movement. Margarete solemnly confirms the story, citing the testimony of a friend of hers in Jena who was present at the wedding ceremony.

Distraught, and unable to make contact with Thilo himself, Inge increasingly takes refuge in the sympathetic companionship of her new friend, Stefan Vogel. The quietly supportive attentions of this young man have already won her affection, so that when the bolt from the blue arrives – Thilo's arrest and sudden marriage – his friendship assumes a new importance.

What follows does so with a rapidity that feels at once exhilarating and utterly out of step with any real developments in her heart. The latter will come in their own time, she tells herself. Meanwhile, she finds it strangely pleasurable to violate the delicate mechanism of her own emotional nature; to subvert or even destory the Inge Leibus on whom the pain of rejection by the one man she has ever loved has been inflicted.

One Saturday, on a perverse whim, she suggests to Stefan that they go to the horse races, something she has never had the slightest interest in doing before now. Ever obliging, Stefan takes the S-Bahn with her out to the Hoppegarten Racetrack. They sit together in the sunny freshness of the spring day, high up in the red brick grandstand, with a copy of the *Rennkurier*, picking out horses for each other to bet on. The racetrack has a pleasantly raffish atmosphere. With its smells of sweat and beer and horse dung, not to mention the distinctly uncommunist financial activities permitted to take place within its precincts, it gives one the feeling of having been released into a tolerant, almost relaxed universe. This isn't of course the case, as the large number of purple-trousered Soviet officers strolling about with their girlfriends testifies, but even this sanctioned, illusory freedom raises the spirits. And perhaps because the horses themselves, by their sheer vividness and grandeur, succeed in temporarily ousting any civic agency from the centre of one's consciousness, it allows one to occupy one's body as an animal of flesh and blood for a moment, rather than as a 'citizen' or a 'comrade'.

A fraught joy takes hold of Inge. The pain of Thilo's disappearance continues to ache inside her, but over it a thin euphoric sheen appears to have formed. Impulsively, she puts her hand on Stefan's shoulder and brushes his cheek with her lips. He laughs his quiet, serious laugh.

'Choose another horse for me,' he tells her.

'All right.'

She picks a name at random; a rank outsider. He goes down, places the maximum stake: ten marks. A little later she's gripping his hand tightly, as they watch the horse thundering past its rivals into the final stretch.

'I'll take you out to lunch' Stefan offers, fanning the winnings in his hand.

They lunch at the Müggelturm Restaurant, Inge ignoring her heaped plate of steak and mushrooms in favour of the sweet Bulgarian wine, gazing with increasingly heavy-lidded eyes at the sleek faces of the party functionaries and their pampered-looking mistresses feeding around them.

'What am I doing here?' she murmurs. Stefan smiles gravely, takes her hand across the table, squeezes it gently, brings it to his lips with a look of tentatively ironic gallantry and plants a kiss on it. She smiles, feels a pang of longing for Thilo that threatens to spill over into a sob, and swallows it back down with a gulp of syrupy wine.

'Take me home, Stefan.'

As they walk arm in arm down the street, they pass one of the *Exquisit* boutiques where imported luxuries are sold for Western currency. As with the racetrack and the restaurant, Inge has never before entered such a place. In the high-minded world of her father's home and the peace movement, it is second nature to believe that the one thing worse than failed communism is successful capitalism.

But after all, she has just been betting on the horses, hasn't she; getting half drunk at a well-established symbol of the hypocrisy of the higher echelons of the party; and wasn't it Thilo himself who told her to forget about politics? All right, then: so be it. Let the cup of degradation be drunk to its dregs! They slow to a halt at the entrance to the boutique, then wander in together without a word.

The goods – heavy binoculars and cameras, thick crystal bottles of perfume, lustrous Italian shoes and ties – have a charged presence unaccounted for by their ostensible function. Bathed in the brownish light of their display cases, they seem to her like ceremonial objects from some occult religion. In her heightened state, she feels as though she has entered the force field of some immense and distinctly sinister power. She touches the black lamb's-wool collar of a short, beautifully tailored coat made of green suede. A little to her surprise she sees that it is communist-built rather than Western: *Interpelz*, the label reads. Down some new conduit of thought, opened no doubt by the Bulgarian wine, runs the somewhat chimerical idea that this, unlike the Western items, would be an acceptable possession; that it represents not the familiar idea of luxury based on exploitation and exclusion, but a token fetched back from some egalitarian utopia of the future, where everyone will be dressed in such a coat, and that to own it would merely be to assert one's faith in such a future.

'Why don't you try it on?' she hears Stefan say.

'Don't be ridiculous! Look how much it costs.' She holds the price tag out to him.

'Try it on anyway. I'd like to see how you look.'

With an apprehensive glance at the store clerk, Inge slips off her flimsy anorak and swims her hand down the fleece-lined sleeves of the coat. It fits perfectly, gloving her long-armed torso like a second skin, the collar soft against her neck.

'My God, you're beautiful,' Stefan murmurs. The words seem to come from him involuntarily. He is gazing at her in what appears to be a state of mesmerised admiration. It makes her a little uncomfortable, but also – she has to admit – excited. For a moment, as though trying on a new person-ality along with the coat, she finds herself imagining what it might be like to be the powerful partner in a relationship, the object of such an intense, helpless-seeming veneration.

'I think you should look in the mirror,' Stefan says.

She hesitates.

'Come on, have a look.'

An odd habit of hers, inculcated in her at an early age, is to avoid looking in mirrors.

'Come on, it won't hurt you,' he whispers again with a grin. And in the spirit of wilful self-desecration that has been upon her all day, she moves with him across the floor to the full-length mirror.

'How about it?'

She looks in the mirror. As always on reacquainting herself

141

with her appearance, she has the troubling sense of being confronted by a competing destiny: a happy, thoughtless existence based on physical beauty. The chic cut and glamorising detail of the coat seem to pull her almost irresistibly into this glazed, alternate image of herself.

'I don't care for it.' Brusquely, she pulls her arms out of its sleeves and hangs it back on the rack.

'Let's go,' she says more softly, taking Stefan's arm and leaning into him, 'you were supposed to be taking me home.'

They move back out into the pale afternoon air.

There should be a word for this, she thinks, this processional journey of two people walking through grey city streets to a house where they know they are going to make love for the first time. She is aware that, however little premeditation she may have given it, she has amply signalled her readiness for this, and that Stefan, in his tactfully low-key way, is already in the process of making the mental transition from companion to lover. There is a quiet purposefulness about him as he walks beside her – an appearance of inward preparation. For her own part, she finds herself moving in and out of the reality of what has begun to unfold. One moment the heavy sweetness of impending desire fills her, bringing with it a sense of darkly consoling oblivion. The next she feels utterly detached.

The house she's living in is a clean-scoured, semi-legal squat with a floating population comprised mainly of members of the women's peace movement. There's a sound of voices from the communal downstairs rooms when she and Stefan arrive.

'Let's go up,' she says quietly.

As they climb the uncarpeted wooden stairs to her attic room, she feels again the sting of Thilo's remark that she should forget about politics. Her life in this house has been nothing *but* politics – one long, heated conversation that has made its way through the introduction of female military conscription, the forming of peace workshops, the forging of links with Western anti-nuclear movements, and on to the more recently engaged topics of pollution, eco-activism . . . Is Thilo accusing her of faking her interest in all this? And the actions she has taken part in – the Dresden rally back in '82 where they put candles on the Liebfrauenkirche in defiance of that toadying bishop's orders; the big provocation a year later when Petra Kelly came over the Wall with her West German Greens and they all unfurled banners together in Alexanderplatz until the cops came and arrested them; the time she helped out a friend of Thilo's who'd smuggled a matrix printer in from the West, persuading her housemates to let him hide it under the floorboards of the attic room, where it still lies, a great dense slab of glowering illegality – is he telling her that this was all somehow fraudulent too?

A by-product of her sympathetic attentiveness to other people is that her initial response to criticism tends to be outright acceptance. This can involve a radical (if only temporary) adjustment in the way she inhabits her own mind: a kind of privately performed impersonation of the alternative Inge that her critic seems to be proposing. *What if he's right?* she asks herself. *What if I only took part in those things because the people I admired, principally Thilo himself, were doing them, and I wanted to impress them?* The possibility comes to her that rather than falsifying her nature with Stefan all day today, she has in fact been doing precisely the opposite: casting off certain grandiose pretensions, and reverting to her true essence: that of an actress; hopelessly shallow and chameleonic. *Vain too*, she adds for good measure.

As they step into the tiny, mirrorless room, she closes the

door behind them and stands still, waiting to see what Stefan will do.

He smiles at her. His eyes are a stony blue, grained with yellow. A small dimple in his chin emphasises the somewhat bland symmetry of his face, but gives it a nice boyishness too. One thing she definitely could not handle at this moment would be some brawny, hairy-shouldered specimen of feral masculinity. Stefan's slight frame and unassertive physicality seem to demand minimal internal adjustment and threaten minimal disturbance. He takes her hand in his, and with only the slightest sense of being brought across the threshold of her own psyche, she finds herself being kissed gently on the mouth.

With Thilo, lovemaking has – *had* – always a fraught, almost traumatic quality, articulating both their passion for each other and their almighty struggles against their own possessive instincts. Every caress seemed pressurised, wrung into a state of high tension, by those contradictory forces. In its tumultuous way it was an illumination as well as a catharsis, but it tended to leave her feeling shattered too, and in the wake of it she was often left with the troubling sense that she might not, in the final analysis, be a match for Thilo.

This is child's play by comparison. The arousal of desire, the disrobing, the entangling of their naked bodies as they lie down on the narrow metal bed, even the statutory pause for the prosaic matter of protection – all proceed with a friction-less simplicity that feels new to her. It has crossed her mind that Stefan might be an inexperienced lover, that she might find herself having to lead the way, but he seems to know what he wants, and in the absence of any conflicting or clearer wants of her own, she becomes ungrudgingly acquiescent. The flat outward gaze of his eyes feeds with evident delight on the surfaces of her body. She is grateful for his apparent ease with the situation. By letting it stand in her mind as the official reaction to it, she is able to marginalise her own *unease* to the point where it becomes almost imperceptible.

As she tightens against him, matching his steady movements with her own, she begins to feel less like a human being than a machine: a precision-built, pleasure-feeling automaton, effortlessly going through its paces with another of its kind.

And it is no doubt precisely by association with this absence of effort, this unaccustomed, frictionless ease, that the fateful word she utters unthinkingly after they finish precipitates itself out of the drowsy vapours of her mind, idling across her lips as she lies sleepily on his bare shoulder:

Amerika.

'America,' she hears herself murmur.

'America?'

'America's where I'd want to go if I ever left this country. I wouldn't go – I wouldn't go anywhere German.'

'Oh? Why's that?'

She stares up through the rain-grimed skylight.

'I would want to be in another universe, without any connection to this one, not even the language. Maybe that more than anything . . .'

'Oh, yeah?'

'I could work there too. I have a director friend who comes here sometimes. He's always saying he wants to put me in one of his films . . .'

'That's very interesting . . .'

The tone of Stefan's voice is casual, but with her ear against his chest she can hear that his heart has exploded into life. After a long silence, she feels him clear his throat.

145

'What if I could get you there?'

'I'm sorry?'

'What if I could get us to America?'

'How could you possibly do that?'

'Vitamin B.'

'Huh? Oh . . .'

It takes her a moment to translate the rather dated slang. 'You have connections?'

'Yeah.'

'I didn't know that.'

'I think I could get us exit visas . . . I mean, with you being a known artist. Would you go?'

Again, the tone is casual, but under it she can feel the stirring of what appears to be a large preoccupation.

'Would you?' Stefan urges.

'I don't know.'

He sits up, gazing down at her with a strange vehemence. An uncharacteristic wildness glitters in his eyes.

'Listen to me, Inge. I'll tell you something. I'm in love with you. I don't know if you feel that way about me. But it's not out of the question that it could happen, right? I mean, you quite like me?'

She nods. No objection there.

'Well, what I'm saying is there's no future here. Not even the remotest possibility of happiness. You know that, don't you?'

'Do I?' she answers. 'Maybe I do.'

'So if we can get out, then don't you think – I mean, why stay?'

She looks up, saying nothing. He kisses her mouth, brushing the back of his hand over her breasts. The subject seems to have rearoused him. She smiles, feeling a bemused, almost

146

vicarious pleasure as he caresses her. His excitement makes her want to cheer him on. It's certainly nice to be so unequivocally wanted by someone. And again, in the absence of any clear sense of what she herself wants any more, she can feel the attraction of simply docking onto some desire larger than anything in her own heart and cutting herself adrift.

'So would you?' he asks again. 'Would you come?'

'I – I'd have to think about it.'

'*Will* you think about it?'

The image of herself in one of her old friend Eric Lowenthal's movies insinuates itself briefly through her defences. Hadn't Eric always told her he'd do anything to help her if she ever came West? Privately, or at least in the part of herself that she has hitherto shared only with Thilo, she has always despised Eric's films a little: simplistic moral tales featuring second- or third-world miseries sentimentally repackaged for first-world consumption. But now that Thilo has so irrevocably repudiated her, perhaps it is time to reconsider: step into that alternate existence she glimpsed earlier in the mirror; wrap herself in the mystique of foreignness and exile, let Eric turn her into one of those glamorous stars of 'independent' cinema he had become so adept at manufacturing . . . A sham, no doubt, but not a bad life, perhaps; turning one's back haughtily on photographers at Cannes, making the odd surprise appearance out of a taxi or limousine at gala charity events for the more austerely worthwhile causes . . .

'Will you think about it, Inge?'

'OK.'

'Do you promise me?'

'Yes, Stefan. I promise.'

CHAPTER 13

Insidious way in which the habits of one's life reassert themselves — even just the habit of pottering about, not thinking or feeling anything very much at all.

I pay bills, I make my online trades (I shorted Intel again — made almost two thousand dollars), I walk Lena, I've even been splitting and stacking firewood for winter . . .

Meanwhile, I think less and less about my drenching at Gloria's party, and when I do, I find myself wondering if I wasn't making altogether too much of it in the first place. It begins to seem almost possible my assailant was just some unhinged or drunk woman who happened to overhear Gloria introducing me to Harold Gedney, and attacked me for no better reason than that she objected to my name or didn't like my face. I can believe that one's deeds leave their signature in one's outward appearance; that for those with eyes to see such things, a person's more significant actions may be legible in the cast of their features or some cryptic singularity in their gait. In other words, that the woman's violence was motivated by an act of impersonal clairvoyance rather than any actual connection to my own past.

At any rate, with every day that goes by I feel less impetus to rock the becalmed boat of my existence, let alone outright incriminate myself.

Logically, I should therefore abandon this memoir. What purpose in an incomplete account of things; a promise of disclosure that turns out to be an act of concealment?

And yet, having come this far, I find myself just as reluctant to stop as to go on. It may be that this is nothing more than the same condition of inertia that afflicted me during my adolescence: one of those 'Dragons of Stability' stationed at the valve of memory, ensuring that any attempt to close it will require more effort and decisiveness than leaving it open. Possibly; but I sense something else too: some fractionally more positive, or at least aesthetically compelling, reason for continuing, having to do with a suspicion that our arrival in America sixteen years ago may in fact be more accurately evoked with the veil still drawn over the events immediately preceding it than otherwise.

That, after all, was how I experienced those first years: as a time of total division from the past. Hadn't we come to the New World in order to build new lives for ourselves? Were we not entitled – even by a certain logic *required* – to leave all the fault and failure of our old lives behind us? What had happened in our prior lives no longer concerned us, I told myself. It was henceforth eternally sealed off from the present, just as the place in which it had occurred was sealed off eternally (so I believed) from the place we were in now. And in fact I pictured the mental barrier I had constructed between present and past as a wall just as solid and impregnable as the physical wall running through my home city.

I remember those first months of ours here in the States as a period of unbridled revelation and joy. I was like a tropical plant kept for years in a cold climate, then transported to its ancestral soil and suddenly budding with unexpected new life. From the moment we drove in from the airport and took possession of our fifth-floor apartment (tiny and bare but looking out on the vivid bustle of the East Village), I felt things stirring in me: new powers, new facets of spirit, heart, appetite . . . I was freed, awakened; I felt at the threshold of a most sunlit existence.

It was 1986: another era, it seems now; its ruling principle that of contrast: violent, abrupt and shameless. One moment we were turning out the lights in the church-run homeless shelter below us, with its single grimy sink for all twelve inhabitants; the next we were arriving at one of Gloria Danilov's parties with their caviar wagons and salvers of pink smoked salmon.

Both sides of the picture fascinated me: the ruin and the glamour. I came at them with an undiscriminating hunger that each aspect seemed to satisfy equally. I liked the grime and the grunge, the filthy subway cars lurching by in a fluorescent lichen of graffiti, the street-cleaning vehicles whirling their medieval-looking brooms over the crack vials and sodden porn mags of the East Village gutters. These things had a power about them despite their ungainliness; a lumbering industrial potency that their equivalents in the GDR had never possessed in my eyes. It was just an orientation in the direction of purpose, I suppose, but even that was new to me; the reverse of the machines I had used during my stint in the Construction Brigade, where a comprehensive cynicism was detectable in every malfunctioning switch and lever. I felt immediate affection for the starkly elemental street furnishings: the trash baskets, meters, hydrants, all cast in the same lava-grey substance that looked like metal regressing to its stone ore. The tenements opposite us with their pirate-ship riggings of fire escapes, their water silos bristling like fat, primeval rockets, had a fantastical grandeur in my eyes, as

150

did the empty lots in their chain link and razor wire, where spindly ailanthus trees grew out of the enormous mounds of garbage. And though it frightened me, the darkness of the project blocks by the East River, where the street lamps had broken and violence seemed electrically imminent as you walked by, filled me with admiration too. To be truthful, my enthusiasm embraced even the human wreckage – the junkies down at the needle exchange office on the first floor of our building; the crack-addicted, AIDS-ravaged figures panhandling in Tompkins Square or curled up on the streets in cardboard boxes; the sidewalk vendors laying out their pitiful bric-a-brac of toothless combs and empty cotton reels . . . All of these sights, which soon began to appal Inge, had an exhilarating effect on me. They seemed to raise the stakes of my own existence; enlarge my sense of what it was to be alive on this earth. I felt wrenched out of the confines of the world I had grown up in, where the spectrum of available experience corresponded so suffocatingly to the tiny size of the country itself. As the old joke there went, a husband suggests to his wife that they spend their vacation taking a tour of the entire GDR. 'Oh, yeah?' says the wife. 'What are we going to do in the afternoon?'

And meanwhile there was the other side of the picture: those visions of pure, dripping gold. Furred models stepping from limos to shop for diamond ankle bracelets; tanning parlours where god-like bodies revolved under ultraviolet lamps . . . Even just the food stores: to behold for the first time those illuminated tiers of fruits and vegetables, the forests of flowers spilling out their scent and colour from the East Village bodegas; to walk on and be confronted, on the same block, by another, then yet another such *Wunderkammer*; to go inside and fill a basket with delicacies you had never bothered to

151

distinguish in your mind from the nectars and ambrosias of myth, so little had you ever expected to taste them; to watch your bill being created by nothing more than the passing of each item over the glass-topped counter's mysterious scarlet ray – all of this was an astonishment to me; one that merely increased as I discovered that these bodegas occupied not the highest but in fact the very lowest position on the city's hierarchy of stores, that above them were the more resplendent Korean groceries with their banked, year-round fires of grapefruit and peach and strawberry, that these in turn were as nothing to the crammed volumes of the Gristedes and D'Agostino chains, which were themselves eclipsed by the mighty cornucopias of Zabar's, Balducci's, Dean & DeLuca, where the entire planet seemed to have concentrated its riches for one's delectation; our own Baltic condensed into a hundred types of smoked fish, the Mediterranean gemmed and gleaming in jar after jar of olives; all of this of course entirely commonplace to other shoppers, but to us as startling as if a New Yorker should walk into a shop and find delicacies from Jupiter and Venus casually on display. And then the buildings themselves, the skyscrapers, my childhood fetishes, rising south and north over the humbler rooftops of the Village: the Empire State like a great syringe with some fiery elixir of the city vatted inside it, the Helmsley in its gold tiara, the Twin Towers reading each other's paragraphs of light . . .

How I loved this place! Having spent my teenage years dreaming of being reborn as an American, I should not have been surprised by this, but the reality of the country so exceeded my wildest imaginings that I would sometimes find myself in a state of almost painfully overfulfilled expectation. Even the shelter we supervised on the floor below us was a source of unexpected joy. I had imagined it was going to be a place of pungent squalor and criminality; that to pass muster there I was going to have to find the resources of a prison guard somewhere inside me. But I was mistaken: the men who lived there, far from being the brutal or broken spirits my anxiety had conjured, seemed to me to embody, in a peculiarly pure form, precisely the qualities I had always most desired for myself: vitality, innocence, hope. Their stripped-bare lives, even the undeniable craziness of one or two of them, elevated them in my eyes, giving them an almost heroic air. I remember them vividly: David, young, lean, furiously energetic on his diet of protein powder and homegrown alfalfa sprouts, a fanatic reader of memoirs by billionaire executives, monopolising the pay phone with his own labyrinthine moneymaking schemes; Donald, bankrupted by medical bills, lumps all over his neck, forever poring over an enormous dictionary, convinced he needed only to master the rules of 'orthography' in order to get his life back on track; Jean-Luc, a qualified doctor (so he claimed) who had come to America from Haiti in search of a job, had his suitcase stolen with all his medical certificates, and been marooned ever since, his kindly eyes signalling, as he told you this, that he didn't expect you to believe a word of it and forgave you in advance for your scepticism . . .

In the evenings, as they drifted in from the streets after we unlocked the door (our principal duty, along with keeping the store-cupboard stocked with laundry soap and toilet paper), I would sit with them in the communal room, spell-bound. Their conversation revolved around two themes, each as intoxicatingly 'American' to my hyperattentive ears as the opening notes of *Appalachian Spring* or some other purebred anthem: their eager willingness to take responsibility for their own predicament, and their unquenchable optimism for the future. They were homeless, they believed, simply as a result of what they called their 'bad choices'. But they also believed that the good life was attainable to anyone in this great country of theirs, themselves included, and that all it required was for them to make, instead of those bad choices, the 'right' choices, which they would make as soon as they were 'ready'. As simple as that! No talk of bad luck or the inherent injustices of the social order; nothing between themselves and their destiny: an apocalyptic nakedness! Every one of them, it seemed, was a millionaire-in-waiting: right now they were just going through their shelter phase, as the heroes of legend go through their obligatory spells in the desert or the pauper's hovel. Absurd as it may sound, I wanted to be as they were: emptied out of everything but faith and hope! Their glamour extended from themselves to the physical space they inhabited. Dingy as it was, with its soiled woollen curtains, calcium-bearded radiators, narrow beds and bits of old carpet remnant, the place had a rock-bottom sufficiency that I found strangely appealing. The hot water worked; the kitchen always had plenty of store-donated food in it; there was company if you wanted it, but no one imposed on you. I remember thinking that if we failed to make a go of things in this city, I, for one, would be content to end up in such quarters.

But there was no reason to believe we would not make a go of things. We had a glamour of our own. We were young, exotically foreign; people wanted to know us; they wanted to help us. My father's old opposite number at the UN, Jim McGrievey, now an attorney in private practice, received me in his midtown office soon after we arrived. A spry, mirthful-eyed man, amused to be in the position of being called on by the son of his old 'sparring partner', he fired a few innocuous questions at me about my life in Berlin. I told him, in the vaguest terms, about my literary endeavours, predicting, correctly, that he would not press me for details. With the innocently satisfied look of a person matching two puzzle pieces together, he leaned over his desk and said to me: 'Listen. I'm going to introduce you to a good friend of mine, Gloria Danilov. She's a wealthy lady – very politically connected but she also likes to have creative people around her. Play your cards right and she'll do something for you, I'm sure of it. Here, I'll have my secretary arrange a meeting right now . . .'

And a week later, by the gliding logic that seemed to govern our lives in those days, I was being shown by a butler into a flower-filled waiting room in a vast residence on Park Avenue. My audience with Gloria lasted no more than a few minutes – delegations of businessmen and politicians were no doubt waiting their turn in other parts of the building – but the brevity of our meeting in the alcove of her library, looking out on the late summer dusty greenness of the park, merely seemed to concentrate its impact on me. I remember the dreamlike strangeness of being addressed as if it were an estab-lished and incontrovertible fact that I was a distinguished Man of Letters and bona fide political dissident. There was no reason, of course, for Gloria to question my credentials: McGrievey would have recommended me in flattering terms, while her own burnishing propensities naturally raised my alleged accomplishments to yet more unrecognisable heights of brilliance. What did surprise me was that, while in the past such credulousness would have made me uneasy, here I found myself fully acquiescing in Gloria's version of myself. It was as if she had some magical power of suspending the true nature of whatever came into her orbit, and persuading it to conform with her preferred vision of things.

As we were talking she placed her large, warm hand on mine, as though we had been the dearest of friends for many years.

'I want you to help me with my magazine,' she said. 'I want you to help me choose the unsolicited pieces we sometimes run. I've been looking for someone with a more international perspective than our intern who does it at the moment. You're *just* the person I have in mind. Will you do it for me?'

I accepted without hesitation: her belief in me seemed to obliterate my own knowledge of what I was. The job, a virtual sinecure, gave me a pleasant office I could wander into whenever I had nothing better to do, a stipend of a thousand dollars a month, and – more precious to me than anything – the satisfaction of being a cog in the mighty, humming machinery of my new world.

Meanwhile, Inge too seemed to be in the process of establishing a new life for herself. Eric Lowenthal, true to his word, had chosen his new project with her in mind, and he began developing it soon after we arrived. He made a tremendous fuss over both of us, and seemed to want to convey that he considered Inge a great prize, going out of his way to include us in every part of the immense effort involved in getting the project off the ground. Every week there were lunches with producers and investors. There were late-night sessions watching audition tapes at his Tribeca apartment. There were rides out of the city to scout locations; script conferences where Eric would consult us on his latest revisions; meetings with lawyers, agents and distributors . . .

Again that purposefulness, so utterly novel to me; the sense that one's inner desires and dreams could actually be transformed into material realities in this miraculous new universe.

At first, Inge seemed to thrive in its bracing atmosphere as much as I did. A rehearsal period had been set for the following spring, with shooting to start early that summer. The film – a sort of philosophical parable, I gathered – was about a poor émigré from Poland who cleans houses in New York and finds herself inexplicably beset by wealthy American admirers. 'You've read *Being and Time*, of course?' Lowenthal had said to me in an attempt to explain it. I had nodded (though I hadn't read a word). 'Well, think of Inge's role as the "Remembering of Being", and the men wooing her as supplicants trying to recover that memory.' Which meant nothing at all to me, though Inge appeared to approve, which was all that mattered. Already by winter she was beginning to submerge herself in her role, and as the rehearsal date approached, she seemed to burn again with the same subdued glow of gathering energies (I think of the flames, barely visible in daylight, on jet-fuel refineries in airports), as she had when I first saw her in that Prenzlauer Berg theatre. For a time I even had the sense that she was shifting, with Eric's encouragement, into that other self of hers: the actress/beauty who offers up her mysterious vitalities in exchange for the world's regard.

This was our grace period, in retrospect; our honeymoon. There were tensions, of course; little erratic shock waves from the past; shadows cast backwards from the future. The words '*glasnost*' and '*perestroika*' had begun appearing in newspapers and on people's lips, and they disturbed me, dimly, like obscure portents in a dream. There were problems, right from the start, in Inge's adjustment to the American way of life. The jetsam of squalor washed up every morning by the tides of a free, unsanitised press created special difficulties for her peculiar, somewhat morbidly compassionate temperament.

With no capacity for detachment, no ability to unsnag her heart from the things that caught hold of it, she could be reduced to despair by the contents of the Metro Section of the *New York Times*. Every one of those grim stories – old people frozen to death in trash-filled apartments; children starved, beaten, hit by stray bullets – seemed to lodge itself inside her and take root there, requiring her to enter into every corner and cranny of its pain, even as each day brought in new ones just as bad. For a while she got it into her head that nothing short of actual, practical intervention would do, and in her quietly fanatical way she would try to help: writing letters to editors, government departments, welfare agencies; badgering our own Lutheran benefactors to get involved; signing up for volunteer programmes; going off on subway rides to far-flung housing projects – this white-blond and no doubt utterly baffling foreigner, offering her assistance to complete strangers in her imperfect English . . . Then, as the ineffectuality of her efforts, the massive indifference they met, became impossible to ignore, she shifted her energies towards this more passive act of empathy – *snip-snip, snip-snip* (I can hear her now) – as though instead of trying to relieve the world's suffering, she had settled for the role of its recording angel.

But although the forces aligned against us may have already been stirring, our own springtime surge was stronger than they were. I remember looking out through the window of our apartment one January morning and taking stock of our lives – the shelter, my job at Gloria's magazine, Inge's budding new career, this uncluttered home of ours, the busy street below with its tumult of cars, trucks, skateboarders, shoppers, idlers, deliverymen; all of these things linked together in my imagination and speeding forward in full sail through the brilliant blue Manhattan air – and feeling in some way I never had before that at whatever cost, and on however dubious a basis, I was alive.

CHAPTER 14

Snip-snip, snip-snip . . . My anchoress upstairs at her devotions.

Oh, these scrapbooks of hers!

Snip-snip, snip-snip . . . Some element of survivor's guilt in her fixation on these dismal stories: punishing herself for getting out . . . ?

Snip-snip, snip-snip . . .

Not that it isn't also squarely the act of repudiation it appears to be.

More so than ever, in fact: a distinct sharpening of focus seems to have occurred since the current administration took office. The latest volume was lying open on her desk the other day when I went up to check our insurance policy. The old 'human interest' stories had given way to more explicitly political pieces. There was a report on the rolling back of the Clean Water Act; another on the destruction of coral reefs, with a Bloomingdale's ad for a new line in coral jewellery set pointedly beside it. On the opposite page were articles on the attacks of two years ago: an administration official saying, 'We should flatten a country or two'; a piece recommending torture be legalised for terrorist interrogations; a professor fired for suggesting America 'had it coming'; vigilantes in some suburb attacking homeowners who didn't have flags in their yards . . .

I leafed back, saw a piece comparing the new powers of surveillance permitted under the Patriot Act with those exercised by the totalitarian regimes of the former Eastern Bloc countries. I flinched at this; balked, found myself unable to read on. Hard for me – impossible, really – with all I have staked on my faith in the greatness of this nation, to swallow such a comparison. I need to believe that what de Tocqueville declared of America remains true in spite of everything: 'America is great because she is *good*.'

Snip-snip, snip-snip . . . As if she were methodically cutting away the very ground under my feet!

Apropos of which, a few years ago we were told our refugee status might be questioned if we ever travelled abroad, and we were advised to apply for citizenship. After several months of filling out forms, being fingerprinted, interviewed, having our English tested, we were given a date to go to the US Southern District Courthouse in Lower Manhattan and be sworn in as American citizens.

Inge was noticeably tense on the bus ride down. She had seemed, when we embarked on this process, to accept my presentation of it as a purely practical matter, without deeper implications. Naturally, I was relieved at her lack of resistance: my priority, as ever, was to keep her with me, on whatever terms and at whatever cost, and the more unified the outward circumstances of our lives, it seemed, the less power our internal fault lines had to push us apart. But now all of a sudden, in the face of this imminent rite of passage into a new nationality, her breezy indifference appeared to be faltering. I wasn't altogether surprised, but given that we had come this far, I didn't expect anything dramatic to develop. Still, I kept a watchful eye on her.

At the courthouse, we went up to the ninth floor, joining

the crowd of other initiates outside the oath room. The atmosphere was oddly subdued: none of the festive excitement I had read about in reports of these occasions. People were muttering to their lawyers, talking on cell phones, thumbing their Palm-Pilots: all business. I could feel Inge taking this in, and sensed that it was stoking her misgivings. She stood beside me, more agitated by the minute. I resisted the impulse to try to calm her down, afraid this would make matters worse. The important thing, I told myself, was to get through the ceremony. We could talk about what it meant afterwards.

A US marshal appeared and shepherded us into rows of benches in the wood-panelled oath room. Then a judge entered and gave a speech about the Constitution. It was an enlightened speech, emphasising the importance of tolerating voices of dissent in a democracy, and it seemed to me that Inge ought to be reassured by it. But as we listened I could sense her discomfort growing. Her eyes were darting around the room. I followed her glance, wondering uneasily what she was seeing in the expressionless faces of our fellow initiates. After the judge had finished, he told us all to rise.

'We will now say the Pledge of Allegiance to the flag.'

It was at that moment that Inge fled.

'I'll wait for you downstairs,' she whispered, stumbling past the other people in our pew. Before I could say anything, she simply ran off down the aisle, brushing by the astonished marshal without a word of explanation.

'There's no re-entry, ma'am . . .' he called after her.

I stood there, stunned, sensing at once the momentousness of what she had done; feeling its impact, like an axe blow, on what remained of the connection between us, realising that if I wanted to salvage anything I should go after her, and yet already experiencing that curious retroactive

162

fatalism of mine: the sensation, once again, that this was after all nothing new; that it had *already happened*.

The ceremony ground on without her. I pledged my allegiance along with the rest of the initiates, and swore to bear arms for my new country. I added my voice to a tuneless, droning chorus of the 'Star-Spangled Banner'. I signed my naturalisation certificate, shook the judge's hand, and picked up my crookedly photocopied letter from the president telling me that 'Americans are generous and strong and decent not because we believe in ourselves, but because we hold beliefs beyond ourselves'.

Inge was waiting for me downstairs. She didn't offer an explanation and I didn't ask for one. What was there to say? We had become, literally, foreign to each other.

BUT WHAT I was intending to write before the sound of Inge's scissors distracted me has nothing to do with any of this.

Menzer called yesterday. Klaus Menzer.

Inge was at work. I was in, but didn't pick up. He left a message asking me to call him back. He was here, right here in America. The number he gave had a New York area code, a fact I absorbed with a lurch of dismay. I erased the message without taking it; a futile gesture, I realised even at the time.

My head was reeling. I went out – up to the quarry, Lena trotting ahead of me. Fall in full spate up there. Raspberry-coloured sumacs. Fiery orange creepers running up the radio tower. I sat on the stone seat under the cliff, wondering what he could be doing in this country, and what reason he could have for wanting to get in touch with me – with *me* – after all these years. Impossible to imagine he could be calling out of some impulse of innocent nostalgic sociability; not that coiled and involuted man.

Are you Stefan Vogel? Yes. Splash.

And now Menzer. A second missile coming at me out of the past!

He called again this morning. This time I picked up: didn't want to risk him calling again while Inge was in. He was blandly friendly, chatting casually as if there had been no decade-and-a-half gap since we last spoke, and certainly no convulsions on the world stage worth mentioning. He asked if I had plans to come down to the city any time soon so that we could 'get together'. I made a non-committal answer and attempted to change the subject.

'Are you still writing poetry?' I asked him.

'I really hope you can come down, Stefan,' he replied. 'It would be almost a blast . . .'

I caught at once the old, languid coerciveness in his voice, and sensing I might have more to lose by resisting him than by giving in, I agreed to meet him next week.

CHAPTER 15

I took the early bus down to New York. A beautiful morning. It had rained in the night, then cleared. Light streaming down over the mountains. Cables looping forward between the utility poles, thick and heavy and glittering with gold raindrops like ropes of celestial gossamer. (The strange compulsion to note these things down. About as useful as a corpse growing fingernails!)

I had an hour to kill before our appointment. As I wandered slowly downtown, I became aware of a distinctly cooler appraisal of the city forming at the periphery of my familiar affection for the place.

Or perhaps it was more a kind of double vision, as if I were seeing things through a pair of mismatched spectacles: one lens rose-tinted, the other skewed by a disfiguringly merciless clarity.

Outside the Manhattan Fish Market, where I used to linger admiringly every time I passed, I fell into something like my old marvelling delight. But it seemed unstable now, encroached on by some looming unease that required a deliberate effort to resist. What was this? Inge's scepticism superimposing itself on my own more ardent or gullible view? Some dim sense of raped oceans, poisoned seabeds? Could it have been the customers themselves, my fellow citizens, crowding at the counter to take delivery of their dinners, unaware that their guileless faces, their soft-fleshed bellies hanging before them like gentle, spherical pets, their wallet-waving arms, had by some strange quirk of fate come to form the universal hieroglyph for that blunt, plundering motion by which power avails itself of whatever sustenance it requires? Brandt's gesture, it occurs to me; reaching down inside me for what he wanted. My own too, of course, back in Berlin, helping myself to Inge.

I wondered if it was possible that I had misread this city the first time around; mistaken its apparent vigour for a springtime ebullience when in fact what I was witnessing was the hectic gaudiness of the downward, the catabolic, cycle. The invisible worm, to quote myself, ha, that flies through the night, in the howling storm, hurtling down along the city's cracks and fault lines to the sick heart, *splash!* – these flags everywhere its streaming blood, its autumnal foliage?

Menzer was staying in a loft on Bond Street: tall and narrow with dark alcoves off the far end and a clutter of artworks and plants and mismatched grandiose furniture strewn throughout its immense length. It reminded me strongly of his place off Saarbrücker Strasse; so strongly in fact that as I went in I had the feeling not so much of entering a room as stepping into an aura, an enveloping atmosphere of privileged bohemianism that was apparently inseparable from the man himself.

In his own person too he seemed barely changed: a little thinner, a little greyer; his features drawn a little more tightly, as if by some slowly rotating inner ratcheting mechanism, around the uneven contours of his skull. But otherwise no visible concession to the years that had passed since I had last seen him, and certainly no discernible imprint of trauma from his public disgrace. As if being Klaus Menzer were an eternal proposition, not subject to the laws of mutability and decay that govern the rest of us.

He shook my hand.

'Coffee?'

'Sure.'

He made a pot of coffee in the open kitchen; lifting pans and jars with a droll carelessness; the handling of such humble objects being apparently a somewhat comical anomaly in the life of an eminence such as himself.

The same crumpled suit and drab T-shirt as he had always worn in the past drooped in the same ways over his elongated frame. The same silver-rimmed glasses alternately magnifying and concealing his eyes.

We sat with our mugs in armchairs of padded corduroy and gilded wood. I said little: I had made up my mind not to incur humiliation by engaging Menzer in nervous small talk. I would outsilence him: force him to work his own way towards whatever communication he had summoned me here in order to make. He gave a faint smile, seeming to take note of this, and to be amused by it.

'So. Here we are in America,' he said.

'Yes.'

'How long, for you?'

'Since '86.'

'You must like it.'

'I do.'

'Inge also?'

'Yes.' I had no intention of opening up my private life to him.

'No plans to go back?'

'No.'

He nodded.

'Me neither. I like it here. Did I tell you why I came over?'

'No.'

'Would you like to hear?'

'OK.'

'A film producer wanted to make a movie about me!' He gave a laugh. 'How about that? He brought me over from Berlin earlier this year and we flew to Hollywood together. Have you ever flown first-class? There were little pink shreds all over the bathroom. I thought someone had been tearing up the toilet paper, but it was rose petals! In Hollywood I had a house to myself up in the hills with glass walls looking onto the ocean and a garden full of orange trees. The ocean there isn't blue, which would be almost boring, but sort of a fluorescent violet, with gold sparks on it at night . . .'

I sat back in my baronial chair, sipping my coffee, a little surprised that the great Menzer should think it worth the effort to give me his impressions of Hollywood, but content to hear him out. A chrome lamp hung from a long, snaking stem, its base far away in another part of the enormous room, so that the light it shed on us seemed somehow stolen or siphoned off.

'We had meetings with studio executives every day. Those studios are like fiefdoms from the middle ages – they have their own private armies and transportation systems, their own livery, even their own language. Paramount is the Vatican, hacienda-style. The executives are all from tiny, specialised countries like Iceland or Finland. We sat in their offices and told them my life story. The leader of the Prenzlauer Berg avant-garde poetry scene who turns out to have been a Stasi informer: that was our pitch. They thought it was hilarious.'

Strange sensation – a kind of simultaneous pain and numbness – as he alludes in that matter-of-fact way to his betrayals. As if treachery were just some private habit you could make socially acceptable by coming out of the closet about it; shifting the burden of shame from speaker to listener . . . I tried not to flinch, but Menzer's sensitive antennae picked up my unease immediately. He smiled:

'You were never Gaucked, were you, Stefan?'

'What?'

He spoke quietly. 'Your file was never opened, was it?'

'Not to my knowledge,' I replied. I refrained from adding that I imagined he already knew that.

'What I thought,' he said.

He paused, the sign of some sort of delicate quandary appearing on his expressive face. That face! Under our cone of light every tilting plane in it, every meandering gully seemed brimmingly inhabited by him; the dwelling place in which some particular refinement of his elaborate spirit was lovingly housed, like the different parts of an instrument in its plush-lined case.

'Well. To get back to my movie . . .' The story began unfurling from him once again. I supposed now that he must have some purpose in telling it to me in such detail, that it was not merely a preamble to something else, and I began listening with a sort of guarded attentiveness.

Despite the enthusiastic responses, the meetings had come to nothing:

'They all had the same problem,' Menzer said, smiling. 'They loved the idea but in the end they couldn't see a way to present someone who betrays all his friends as a "sympa-thetic" character; someone audiences can "root for", whatever that means . . .'

Back in New York the producer had settled Menzer's

169

account at the Pierre, where he had been putting him up, and moved on to other projects. But instead of going back to Germany, Menzer had decided to stay on in New York.

'I'm like you,' he said. 'I like it here. I want to stay.'

His plan, he told me, was to try to get this film of his off the ground by himself, as an independent production.

'So I don't get my million dollars,' he said, with a shrug that managed to convey both an unabashed sense that he was owed such a sum for his life story, and a princely indifference to being deprived of it. 'But from what I hear you can still do all right with these New York companies who make lower-budget films where you don't have to *root* for the hero. Now, this director Inge worked with; the one who used to visit us in Berlin?'

'Eric Lowenthal?'

'Lowenthal. Yes. I was thinking, since he has this prior interest in things East German, he was someone I should maybe get in touch with . . .'

For a moment now I began to wonder whether I had seriously misgauged Menzer. Though I hadn't formed any precise idea of what his reasons for bringing me here might be, I had invested them with a degree of malice in proportion to my belief in the man's limitless capacity for harm. And yet here he was with apparently nothing more sinister in mind than to hustle me for Inge's old connections in the film business!

'Well . . .' I said warily, 'that might not be a bad idea . . .'

'So I was wondering if you thought Inge would be willing to give him my proposal.'

I answered carefully, half daring to hope that if I could placate him in this minor practical matter, I might after all be able to prevent any more menacing demand from entering his mind; half suspecting that this entire apparent reversal of our usual roles, with him as supplicant and myself as potential benefactor, was merely another way of amusing himself at my expense.

'Yes . . . I think she would. I'm sure she would . . .'

It didn't seem the right moment to mention that Inge and Lowenthal had ceased to be on speaking terms many years ago.

'What about the money side?' Menzer continued, casting off another of his disconcerting half smiles into the darkening room. 'Do you think she would be able to put me in touch with investors?'

'Inge?'

'Yes, Inge.'

'Well . . . possibly . . . I mean, I . . .'

As I was blustering, he yawned suddenly and looked at his watch:

'Just a moment.'

Then, to my surprise, he called out towards an alcove at the far end of the room:

'Lilian, it's four o'clock.'

A woman emerged from the alcove. A lover, I supposed. A pang went through me. Had disgrace taken *nothing* from him? His old arrogant manner still intact, this choice piece of Manhattan real estate at his disposal and now, to cap it all, some girl, no doubt adoring as they always were, with nothing better to do than wait around in his bedroom in the middle of the afternoon? She came towards us in the dark room, picking her way through the bric-a-brac like a deer through trees; moving on past the freestanding kitchen. Just before her features came into the light of our chrome lamp, I realised, with the body's quicker apprehension than the mind's, who she was.

171

She came to a halt at Menzer's shoulder, looking at me with an empty expression.

Without her pearls, without the glamorous atmosphere of Gloria's party, without the sting of Harold Gedney's snub still reverberating inside me, she seemed a less imposing figure than my memory had made her. Even so, I felt stunned, caught badly off my guard. And as though she had just thrown her glass of wine at me again I felt a burning sensation spreading down across my face and chest.

'This is Lilian,' Menzer said, 'she's studying design at Parsons. She has to go to class now. Right, honey?'

'Right.'

'See you later. Be good.'

He squeezed her hand and she left, smiling as she passed me by.

A silence ensued after she closed the door. Menzer seemed to be lost in a reverie of private delight at his little *coup de théâtre*, while for my own part I was so shaken I didn't trust myself to speak. I wonder now how I could have failed to see beforehand that my drenching at Gloria's party was connected to Menzer's reappearance out of the blue by more than just the vague fatefulness to which I had attributed both things. Not that it makes much difference what form or combination of forms one's designated Furies assume when they awaken. All that matters is that one recognise them, and even I was capable of that.

It was Menzer who finally broke the silence.

'I thought you'd appreciate the allusion,' he said, smiling, 'as a fellow poet.'

I managed to muster a more or less dignified terseness:

'I missed it.'

'Ascalaphus. The dead man splashed by Proserpine for informing on her. You a *Sinn und Form* poet too!'

'How did you know I'd be at that party?'

'At the museum? Lilian's old roommate told us. She's a friend of Gloria Danilov's social secretary. She –'

But I suddenly didn't care:

'What do you want?'

He feigned bafflement at the question. I rephrased it:

'How much money do you want?'

'Oh, you mean for my movie?'

'Whatever.'

'Well, let's see, I was thinking of offering individual shares to potential investors at five thousand dollars apiece. How does that sound?'

I absorbed this, struck by the realisation that what I was encountering here was one of the abiding motifs of my existence: that act of predation I had been thinking about earlier; the actual naked plundering motion in which a human being becomes for a moment demon-like. I looked at Menzer; peered into his face, into the light-dashed lenses over his eyes, half expecting, hoping even, to catch some outward sign of transfiguration, if only to see how I myself had appeared when I had put the demon mask over my own face.

There was no visible change, of course.

'It's sort of fascinatingly expensive, isn't it, New York?' he was saying, evidently immensely pleased with the way things had gone. 'I have this fantasy –'

'How about fifteen thousand?' I interrupted him again. An idea had come to me. It had just seemed to spring up fully formed out of that fast-moving, dubiously inventive region of my mind, my sprinter's imagination – absurd, outrageous,

173

unconscionable, and yet in its very preposterousness, irresistible.

Menzer looked as if he were trying very hard not to show surprise.

'Five thousand when I get home,' I said, 'then another ten if you do something for *me.*'

A mirthful gleam came into his eye, as though the thought that I should have things in my humble life of such apparent momentousness entertained him greatly.

'Do what?' he asked.

I told him. He listened in silence, and made no comment when I had finished.

'Take it or leave it,' I said, and got up to go. He remained seated, grey and gaunt in the surreptitious light of the chrome lamp.

'Let me think about it,' he said as I opened the door.

'I'll call in a few days,' I told him as I let myself out.

'Inge has a lover,' he called out suddenly. 'Is that what we're talking about here?'

I turned to him, struck by the inadvertant poignancy of this.

'Yes, as a matter of fact it is.'

CHAPTER 16

It's two o'clock, a clear day with particles of ice glinting in the air all the way across the valley. I'm sitting on the stone bench at the quarry in a grey wool coat and fawn-coloured hat with the flaps down over my ears. Lena is in the house; I didn't want her with me. On my lap is a new notebook. The ones I have already filled are in an envelope on the kitchen table with Inge's name on it. At five thirty Inge will come home from her shift at the health food store. If she starts reading right away, she should finish around seven. By that time it will be dark.

The trees are mostly bare now. Everywhere a greyness and a puffiness. Woolly spoor-heads of coltsfoot. Dead goldenrod, the yellow burrs dusty and whitish, stalks black-spotted, mildewy.

Am I afraid? Yes: but in a narrow, purely physical way; the fear concentrated in the back of my neck, from which gossamer-like feelers seem to have stretched all the way up to the clifftop behind me, sending little shock waves back down at every rustle or breath of wind.

I remember when we first came here. Lowenthal's film had ended in fiasco. Shooting had been delayed twice, and by the time it finally started, Inge's brief moment of unalloyed happiness in our exile had passed. Already she had embarked on

175

her melancholy rebellion against our new life, and this, alas, included the film.

From the start she was ill at ease on the set: distracted, withdrawn, her performance erratic. She seemed under a strange compulsion to fail, spectacularly and in public; almost as if to turn herself into a living reproach against the whole enterprise. It didn't help that this period coincided with the time of her 'mercy missions' around the city. Aside from making her frequently late, these expeditions left her too shattered to reimmerse herself in her role with any conviction. Having been dressed in her house-cleaning outfit and made up and brought onto the set, she would stand with her mop or vacuum cleaner in front of the rolling camera looking utterly lost, as if she really were some hapless Polish cleaning lady who had wandered accidentally onto a film set, then turn apologetically to Lowenthal, who, patient to a fault, would cut, give her time to collect herself and call for another take, only for the same thing to happen again, and then again . . . To watch someone sabotage herself is painful under any circumstances; in the concentrated glare and scrutiny of a film set it was unbearable.

I wanted to help, naturally. At Lowenthal's request I came every day to the location. He stationed me beside him at the black and white video monitor, and between shots he would ask me in private what I thought was going on in Inge's mind. I was mesmerised by the grainy, dream-like images of my wife on the little screen, though what I saw in them had little to do with her acting. Like Dr Serkin's X-rays, they seemed to illuminate a state of affairs I had so far managed to conceal from myself. The depth of uncomprehending anguish in them caught me off my guard. It seemed to me my own marriage, and the actions that had brought it about, were being revealed to me with a stark, accusing brilliance. And like those slender trees I used to gaze at in the derelict garden near our apartment in Berlin, they brought back all my old feelings of longing and exclusion: that sense of another universe, bordering intimately on my own, yet impenetrable, and all the more painfully so for the fact that it was now officially in my possession.

None of which would have been any use to Lowenthal, even if I could have summoned the candour to tell him.

The shoot went grimly on, the economics of such enterprises apparently making it impossible to abort them and put everyone concerned out of their misery. By the end the producer was openly predicting the film would go straight to video without a theatrical release. He was right.

And meanwhile I had problems of my own. Those two words that had started popping up everywhere like a pair of fashionable Russian performance artists – '*glasnost*' and '*perestroika*' – had turned out to be more like harbingers of the apocalypse. The world I had grown up in had started collapsing before my eyes. My gathering, dream-like horror as one state after another fell: Poland, Czechoslovakia, Hungary, Romania . . . That sense of some monumental dam – solid as a mountain range, one had assumed – suddenly spouting leaks here, bursting out in torrents there, crumbling, exploding; the pent-up waters spilling out in a year-long jubilant frenzy of rebellion, cascading week after week over TV screens and magazine covers . . . The ghastly comedy of being the one person in the Western world unable to rejoice. Being obliged – in my capacity as one of Gloria Danilov's 'dissidents' – to feign the triumphal delight of a man whose solemn principles had been vindicated, when all I could think of was that this was nothing but some cruel cosmic joke directed at

177

me, me personally: that the very freedom for which I had paid so dearly was all along destined to have been *given* to me, gratis . . . Not to mention the creeping realisation that with every day's opening up of secret archives and locked files, the 'pledge' I had written out and signed – that little devil's bargain I had made on the presumption that it was to be kept in utter darkness for ever – was steadily being approached by this tide of light, that it was merely a matter of time before my black hour was made incandescently public . . .

So that I was suddenly eager to go and bury myself somewhere out of sight of prying eyes.

Inge had never cared for the city, and at this point needed no persuading to leave. We bought an old car and drove up here. It was winter; two feet of snow on the ground. We found the house through an ad in the *Aurelia Gazette*. Our landlord lent us snowshoes and took us up into the woods – my first excursion into the American wilderness.

The sky above the trees was a dark fluorescent blue. Where the sun came through, the melted and refrozen snow crust gleamed like marble. Fallen trees raised its surface in long, smooth veins. A huge icicle fell from the quarry cliff as we passed, hitting the frozen pool with a wondrous tinkling crash. Then the staggering immensity of this view across the valley. Not a road or dwelling or any other construction visible beyond the transmission tower directly below us (and even that in its lace of frost-flowers more like some outcropping of the rocks than anything man-made), so that you had the sense of gazing back into some prehuman world utterly unconnected to this one.

Astounding, humanless purity of it all! The suspicion I had that what I had been hungering for all my life; what, with my limited terms of reference, I had named 'America' – that concentration of unbounded delight and freedom – was something perhaps not human at all, was possibly even incompatible with the condition of being human, and that entering into it might in fact require precisely this: the annihilation of oneself.

Self-destruction: 'the beginning of all philosophy'. Some other *Denker* I had to read at Humboldt. My obscure sense, whenever contemplating this particular act, that far from being a gesture of despair, it is actually one of extreme optimism. I think of Dr Serkin's reversed tarot cards. My life force – my *élan vital*, as he called it – passing, for tactical reasons, as its opposite . . . Not a desire to be dead, but to be differently alive: to be rid of a parasitical second self that has so encumbered one's spirit only the most radical surgery can remove it. One knows, rationally, that such surgery must result in the death of the patient, but that isn't the point of it at all, and the bulk of one's mind persists in regarding the extinction as a side effect; regrettable, of course, but not to be confused with the real goal: the smashing through into a new, clear, unburdened state of being. The dead man's grab at life!

TWO THIRTY-FIVE. Clouds filling up with yellow light, their underbellies grey. A smell of fermenting apples on the breeze. No reason to hold anything back at this point, and yet I still feel myself resisting. My old habits of silence and secrecy. Smash them!

'. . . Stefan, dear boy. Good of you to come . . .'

Uncle Heinrich, rising with a warm smile from his desk at the Office of the Chief of the People's Police. January 1986.

The room comes back to me in vivid detail – the oak cabinets, the rows of law books, the tin globe, the old-fashioned typewriter that looked like the offspring of a church organ and a halved artichoke – preserving itself in memory as if it knew I should be compelled to revisit it constantly over the years, as I have.

'Look at what I have here!' my uncle says joyously. 'It arrived this morning. It's an advance copy. I knew you'd be terribly eager to see it.'

He hands me the new issue of *Sinn und Form*.

'Isn't that thrilling?'

Inside the magazine are two new 'poems' of mine. Aside from not wanting to lose face after my stupid boast, I had sensed that having work published in a prestigious magazine might help me in my pursuit of Inge. Not that I thought she herself would be impressed by such a coup, or even very interested in it (I was right; she couldn't have cared less), but I felt that it would give me a certain confidence I was lacking; a basis from which to promote myself. It would be a one-off relapse into my old habits, I had vowed, and from the vague nausea filling me there in my uncle's office as I opened the magazine and went through the motions of gazing with grateful pride at my illegitimate offspring on their crisp white sheets, I knew that I was not even going to be tempted to repeat the experiment. With luck it would give me the credibility I needed in the eyes of my new acquaintances in Prenzlauer Berg, but beyond that, the sooner the whole matter disappeared back into the past, the better.

After making polite conversation with my uncle for a few more minutes, I stood up to leave.

'Incidentally,' he said, 'I'd like you to meet a fellow I know, a colleague of sorts. He thinks you could be of some service to him. I told him I was sure you'd be more than willing to help. May I introduce you to him when you have a moment?'

180

No hint of shame or awkwardness as he asked. Even in hindsight, I find it hard to say for sure that he was aware of any leverage he might have acquired over me from the favour he had just done, let alone that he was deliberately exploiting it. If there was any notion of reciprocity operating in his mind, it was simply what was fully permitted by social convention: a harmless favour done, a harmless (in his eyes) favour asked in return. If I had refused him outright he might have been a little taken aback, but perhaps that would have been the end of the matter. Anyway, I myself was still too ignorant of these affairs to grasp fully what he was asking me, and other than the usual instinctive reluctance I felt whenever anybody asked anything of me, I had no particular reason for refusing him.

So, from that little leather-upholstered antechamber to hell I found myself proceeding, a few days later, to the living room of an apartment in the quiet suburb of Hohenschonhausen. It belonged to a Lieutenant Hager, case officer in the Operational Group of Main Department XX, responsible for monitoring and penetrating cultural life and political *Aussteiger* activity in the GDR. A sandy-haired man of forty: red eyelashes, thin-bridged nose, austere mouth; pale, freckled complexion indicative of a certain constitutional delicacy, against which the hair-fine lines under his eyes and at the corners of his lips suggested an opposing effort of disciplined self-fortification. He was married, with a child, a boy of six, who was occasionally present when we met. Our first meeting was to establish that I would be willing, in principle, to work as an *Inoffizieller Mitarbeiter*, an 'unofficial collaborator', and for him to outline the plan of action he had devised for me if I should accept. He made no overt effort to coerce me into accepting, and in fact went out of his way to stress the purely voluntary nature of this service:

181

'Any time you want to stop working for us, Stefan, all you have to do is say that you categorically refuse. That's the official rule. Not all case officers lay it out as clearly as they might. For me it's an essential part of our agreement. Do you understand?'

I nodded. He seemed to be telling me the truth, and yet I had so little sense of there being any choice in the matter that I experienced my acquiescence in it not as something that might or might not happen but as something that had, once again, *already happened*. Still unclear to me whether this feeling was the result simply of an accurate reading of the forces implicit in the situation, or whether it came from some aberrant warp in my own psyche: a willingness to please, manifesting itself inside me as a feeling of irresistible pressure.

Or was there something even more dubious at work in my mind: was I, could I possibly have been, actively interested in the pursuit and destruction of the individual whom Lieutenant Hager wanted me to help him ensnare? Is it possible I was motivated not just by some dim terror of having my fraudulent poetic credentials exposed, but also by an active desire to eliminate a rival?

I am attempting to understand myself here: not to make excuses, but not to fall into the inverse vanity of exaggerating my own misdeeds either. 'It is necessary at all times and in all places to make explicit, to demystify, and to harry the insult to mankind that exists in oneself': Frantz Fanon's words, drummed into us at school. I summon an image of my old self to hold up for examination. I can discern fearfulness in that unformed, boyish face; I can see a lurking, secretive ambition; I can make out all sorts of furtive, inordinate desires, but in truth I can find no sign of actual malice.

On the other hand, I can hardly be an objective judge in this matter, and it seems a little late in the day to be erring on the side of anything other than harshness . . . So, let the accused stand charged with cold-blooded complicity to destroy another human being for his personal gain!

THREE O'CLOCK. Will I hear Menzer's car? I hope not. My state of mind is somewhat precarious. I think I will be able to stay put only so long as it's just a matter of simple obedience to the principle of inertia. Any stimulus requiring an act of will to resist is likely to prove too much.

Of course, it's possible he won't show up. He needed some persuading when I went down to see him again in the city. Not that he had any scruples about the act itself – or if he had, he wasn't going to risk being out-Menzered by admitting to them in the face of my own apparent indifference. But he was concerned about the risks, and even after I had demonstrated how negligible these were – a shot that would cause no alarm, no possible connection between himself and the victim and no imaginable incentive on my part to incriminate either him or, by extension, myself – he remained sceptical.

On the other hand, he clearly needed money. He had insisted I bring my payment in cash, and the sight of this as he glanced into the large envelope I handed him over our café table had an effect on him like a surging current on an appliance: something in him seemed to dilate. Though again, as if to offset any suggestion of being impressed, he immediately put on a hard, businesslike expression.

'Well. Suppose I were to ask you to give me the other ten in advance?'

I had come prepared for something like this, and without hesitation took a second envelope from my bag.

'I'll give you another five,' I told him – the total, as it happened, of what I had been able to cash out of my trading account. 'The rest afterwards.'

He looked thoughtfully at the envelope.

'OK, maybe. But I'm interested in how I'm supposed to know you'll actually give it to me afterwards.'

'I think a better question is how will *I* know you won't keep coming back for more after I do? Who has the most leverage in this situation, after all? Considering the past you and I share.'

He laughed at that, conceding the point.

'What about Inge, though – isn't she going to wonder about your bank balance?'

'I deal with all our finances. She's not interested.'

'All right. OK. Possibly maybe. Listen, though. Not that it's in my interest to say this, but do you really think this is going to solve your problems? With her?'

'I'll worry about that,' I said.

He stared hard at me for some time. Then, abruptly, he shrugged.

'Well, why not? Anything to help out an old pal!'

I gave him the envelope.

'It's almost funny,' he said as we parted company a little later, 'I was always the one who walked off with the marksmanship prize in our Hans Beimler games. Maybe I'm about to discover my true vocation!'

'SO. DID YOU decide on a code name?'

My second meeting with Lieutenant Hager.

184

'How about Sloth?'

'Your school nickname?'

There is very little the lieutenant doesn't know about me. I shrug.

'Well, it's your choice. I'll put it here in the file. You need to write out this pledge, by the way.'

'What's that?'

'That you're working for us entirely of your own free will.'

'OK.'

The boy is present, sitting quietly on the floor, building a windmill out of *Lege*. He and his father belong to an 'Interest Association' devoted to restoring old windmills.

'Here are permits for the journal . . .'

He wants me to launch a sort of *samizdat* journal, modestly risk-taking at first, so as not to arouse suspicion of official involvement, then growing steadily more inflammatory.

'Permit to set text in type. Permit to print. Permit to bind. Permit to distribute up to one hundred copies. Be sure to submit receipts for all expenses. We'll reimburse you every month, with a premium for good work. By that we don't mean gossip or rumour but hard facts, along with evidence that can hold up in court. Our ministry lawyers are very particular about that. Don't rush things: it takes time to get your legend accepted. We want people to see you as a serious editor, willing to take real chances; not just some fly-by-night renegade. We're going to give you your own tail; it'll add to your credibility. Wait, Detlef, that doesn't go there . . .'

He goes over to help his boy with the windmill, working from a photograph, while continuing to talk to me from the floor:

'I often tell people in your situation to think of themselves not only as the agent of the Stasi in the peace movement,

185

but also as the agent of the peace movement within the Stasi. The fact is that although we do make it our business to control this so-called opposition, we're as eager as they are to avoid a direct conflict with the West, and we've recognised right from the start that many of their ideas are worth paying attention to. So you see, we can learn from you. It's just a question of whether one allows that energy to be diverted into wasteful political side issues, or whether one keeps it focused on the immediate pressing danger. Personally I find it a little immoral to be talking about, oh, I don't know, reunification, shall we say, or so-called freedom of expression, or even individual human rights, while enough Pershings and Cruise missiles to incinerate every one of us a thousand times over are being amassed right here on our borders . . .'

He tousles his son's hair, then gets up and returns to his chair, as if reminded by his own calm eloquence of the seriousness of the matter at hand.

'You're wondering what I have to say about the Soviet SS 20s,' he continues with a smile. 'That's all right, we can discuss anything here. Well, I'll tell you: having made quite an extensive study of these things, I can state categorically that the idea of being able to make peace without a credible threat of one's own is a suicidal illusion. We would simply be swallowed up into the capitalist order, where we would incidentally occupy the very lowest rung. Anyone proposing unilateral peace has to be in effect proposing the end of socialism, which means the end of hope for all but the most powerful and predatory groups of people on the planet, and finally of course the end of the planet itself. Which is why certain potential leaders of the movement have to be considered hostile-negative forces. They may be full of noble intentions but unfortunately that doesn't make them any less dangerous. Do you see?'

186

I felt that the lieutenant believed what he was saying; that his words were his own and that he had come to them by his own processes of thought. Unlike my uncle, whose 'innocence' was no doubt largely a matter of an innate disposition to serve the prevailing system as cheerfully and faithfully as he could, Lieutenant Hager seemed to have thought hard about the cause he worked for. He prided himself on his idealism and his moral integrity (the *Lege* set was a case in point: only a zealot would have inflicted that dismal knockoff of Western Lego on his child; most men in his position would have obtained a set of the real thing). His lean, smooth-drawn face, with its lines like fine wrinkles accidentally ironed into a shirt, had a distinctly monkish quality, and I have no doubt that in his own imagination he was playing the role of the hero of conscience, so pure of heart he could engage in activities of a nature that might have tainted a less sterling soul than his own.

And maybe he was right: maybe what was so catastrophically damaging to me was entirely harmless to him. Who am I, after all, to look back at that face and say with such confidence: 'Demon'? What do I have to support this view other than my own sense of injury? History? A dubious ally: suppose its verdict had gone the other way (and after all, it has given the victor's laurels to plenty of questionable causes over time, while cutting off plenty of noble ones before they had a chance to flower); suppose his system had triumphed, flourished into the egalitarian paradise it was all along intended to become, then how would my judgement of the lieutenant itself be judged? With precisely that incredulous scorn we reserve for all those pitiful figures from the past who failed, out of stupidity or narrow-mindedness to perceive which way the wind was blowing.

Blickfeldmassnahmen: our professional term for the act of 'keeping someone in view'.

Abschöpfung: our word for 'pumping'.

I was to keep Thilo Hartman 'in view'. And, in my capacity as editor of a new and daringly outspoken oppositional magazine, I was to look for opportunities to 'pump' him.

THREE FORTY. Bare twigs gleaming like polished wires in the low sun. Lichen on tree trunks showing a gaudy bluish green. A breeze comes down over the clifftop; blows a flurry of yellow leaves off the birches, throwing them out into the lake of air where they spin down, catching the sunlight like gold coins.

Always this feeling of something being conveyed, in some not quite intelligible language, by that other world. Sense of being appraised by the stones, recognised for what I am by the trees. And not just from my *Bausoldaten* days of cutting them down.

This strange yearning they provoke in me! What the ancients had in mind with their idea of the self-slaughtered living on as trees in the afterlife? A projection of precisely this intense desire to sidestep one's own consciousness and merge into the backdrop, the landscape?

That time, right after our marriage, when I almost made a clean breast of things to Inge. Sudden sense, as I turned to her, of the power of words to explode in the air like dynamite, and kill. I kissed her instead.

Inge. Thilo marrying that other woman was out of love for you; you must have half known that: free you from the impossible difficulty of being his lover by trying to make you hate him. Though by the time you figured it out you were

188

here, past the point of no return, while he was – where? In jail? On trial? Alive? Dead? We didn't know: you didn't *want* to know. Your guilt about leaving required you to imagine the worst, and to live as if that were so.

That curious mood of good-humoured resignation he was in during the hour he and I spent together in the little office of my 'magazine'. As though he knew perfectly well there was as much chance that I was in the process of betraying him even as we spoke, as that I was the sympathetic spirit I pretended to be. Choosing, out of what seemed nothing more than sheer gentlemanly magnanimity, to believe the latter, or at least to act as if he did; to respond to my casual probing with such cordial frankness I was left with the sense that even in the part of his mind that must have intuited, in general terms if not precise detail, the wire leading from the pen in my pocket to the transmitter in the heel of my shoe, he bore no ill will, and possibly even forgave me in advance (almost the hardest part for me to bear, that feeling of forgiveness; of being left entirely alone to absorb all reverberation of harm). That moment, after he had shown me the scar on his arm from biting himself in the attempt to master his own feelings of jealousy while you were dutifully following his injunction to 'spend time' with other men; right after that, how I abruptly changed the subject – catch him off his guard, as Lieutenant Hager had instructed me – to the question of the Soviet presence on our soil and then the even more taboo subject of reunification; how, as he gave me his truthful, treasonous answers (handing me his own smiling head on a platter), I felt as though I were traversing a rift in nature, from the far side of which all the previous stumbles and tumblings in my life-long career of falling seemed in comparison to have occurred in a universe of almost childlike innocence!

189

Yesterday I bought a hunting rifle. I wrapped it in plastic and took it up to the top of the cliff. There's an enormous fallen tree there, with several smaller trees splintered and crushed beneath it. Under its torn-up roots is a hole the size of a bomb crater. I climbed down into this and laid the rifle under a ledge of bedrock jutting in through the dirt near the bottom. Menzer has clear instructions how to find it. Assuming he comes (and I am inclined to think he will), he'll park on the old service road for the transmission tower and make his way up the rocky path to the top of the cliff. From there, having found the rifle, he will move towards the edge of the cliff, where, peering down through the birches below him, he will see the mound of bluestone rubble with the stone bench where Inge's 'lover' will be seated, wearing a fawn-coloured hat, looking out at the view as he does every afternoon between four and five o'clock. He will take one shot, which will cause no particular alarm, hunting season having opened today. Then he will go home and wait for me to contact him, which, unless I am seriously mistaken about the nature of what awaits me, will take, as they say here, for ever.

THREE FIFTY. A sheen on the horizon now; a tint of green like a tight-stretched band of silk. What else to set down? I went back a few years ago. Back to Berlin: February of 1999, for my father's funeral. He had died of a blood clot in the cerebellum, while playing chess at his social club.

Otto picked me up at the airport. He and I had kept in touch, though he wasn't much of a correspondent. He'd been struggling, I knew that: divorced, in and out of work, though a couple of years earlier he had turned his military training

190

to advantage, setting up a small garage. A round beard, Amish-style, circled his broad face. It made him look young – the unshaven upper lip – though also prehistoric. He was friendly, a little bemused by me as ever, a little diffident.

'I've thought a lot about you going to America,' he said as we drove. 'I've decided it must have had to do with you being a poet, having the imagination to, you know –'

I turned from him uncomfortably, trying not to listen; watching the rain-blurred parallels of Karl Marx Allee unreel on either side of us, grandiose and relentless. In my head I conducted a shattering conversation with him which would begin with my saying: *Remember those aquavit bottles you got in trouble for stealing . . . ?*

He must have come to an end, as there was a long silence.

'Incidentally,' he said, 'some woman called for you. She wanted to know if you were coming over for the funeral.'

'Who?'

'She didn't say. I gave her the name of your hotel. Figured you wouldn't mind.'

He grinned at me in the mirror, the boyish wickedness of the look confirming my sense of his inviolable innocence. Cord intact. I smiled back, trying to conceal the feeling of alarm that had come into me.

We picked up his children from his ex-wife's apartment, then drove on to his garage. My mother, who was managing the business for him, had insisted on putting in a morning's work before the funeral.

She was on the phone at a metal desk in a chilly office when we arrived; repeating out loud some customer's list of mechanical ailments and typing them into a computer smudged all over with oily fingerprints. She had dyed her hair a coppery auburn colour. Her nails were long and red – the first time I had ever seen them painted. Exhaust pipes were stacked all around her on the cement floor. A stuffed pine marten crouched on the filing cabinet above her, under a calendar with a half-naked girl straddling a tyre. I stood, mesmerised. My mother! Was it possible? Though I had known from Otto's occasional communications that she was working with him, I had pictured the job as something entirely genteel – a little light file indexing that Otto had charitably handed her to keep her occupied; something she might mention to her friends with a glint of irony calculated to express her indomitable spirit in the face of renewed adversity, but certainly nothing harsh enough to account for this apparently wholesale stepping out of character.

'Hand brake slipping,' she said in a croaky voice. 'Power steering broken . . .'

Cradling the phone between her head and shoulder, she typed away with what seemed to me an almost ostentatiously ignoble proficiency. It struck me that she must have wanted me to come upon her like this: *in situ*, soldiering on. Even so, the sight of her in this new incarnation – unprepared as I was by any of the tentative preliminaries that had paved the way towards her earlier transformations – was a shock.

She got off the phone, gave me a brisk, jangling embrace, and at once began talking to Otto about the need to raise prices and increase inventory. *Be advised that we are now members of the mercantile class*, her demeanour seemed intended to convey, *and we don't have the luxury, unlike some people, to think about anything but the immediate material necessities of life.*

Was her briskness an inverted sentimentality? I looked for some sign that being together in the flesh again after all these years was as great an upheaval for her as it was for me, but if it was, she managed to conceal it, and I retaliated with a briskness of my own.

The funeral was brief and low-key, though better attended than I had expected. During the silence in which the coffin was trundled off on its rollers, I heard a strange, raucous sob from the back of the room. Glancing around, I saw a man with tears streaming down his face. A woman beside him began dabbing his cheeks with a handkerchief and patting his hand. It took me a moment to realise that the man was my Uncle Heinrich, and the woman Kitty!

'At least we were able to do that for her,' my mother commented afterwards, as we hurried through the rain to Otto's car. 'Get the social services to pay her to look after him. And to give her credit, she's very patient with him. He's become extremely emotional, as you could see. Not that he would have had a clue who he was weeping for – he just picks up on the atmosphere. Kitty's the only person he recognises now. Everyone else is a stranger he thinks he has to charm each time he meets them. You'll see for yourself, no doubt.'

We drove to Otto's apartment. Kitty arrived with Heinrich soon after us. She threw her arms around me. 'Stefan! I'm so happy to see you!' She had changed remarkably little: same lively grey eyes, same unaffected warmth in their expression. She had qualified as a nurse specialising in care of the elderly, she told me. She was married, to a nightclub manager. They had a boy aged ten. As we talked, the simple creaturely ease of our brief fling came back to me on a warm current of remembrance. I had no wish to rekindle things between us, and nor, I am sure, did she, but I felt an immense gladness that such an interlude had been permitted to occur in my life. Beside her my uncle hung awkwardly, an uncertain smile on his face. Physically he looked in excellent shape: trim and spruce, good colour, his brown three-piece suit as well-fitting on him as the bark of a healthy tree. It was hard to believe there could be anything wrong with him. 'Hello,' I said, offering my hand. He took it, tilting his head questioningly. 'I'm Stefan Vogel,' I told him. He gave a little gallant bow: 'Delighted to make your acquaintance. Isn't this a jolly occasion? Are you a frequent habitué?' I did my best to conduct a conversation with him, aware that for all my belief in his fundamental decency I bore him a great deal of ill will, and that his condition, far from diminishing this, was adding to it a layer of resentment for the fact that he had apparently succeeded in putting himself beyond all possible reckoning. After a few pleasantries had passed between us, a vacant look appeared on his face. He drew close to Kitty, standing behind her for the rest of the reception like a child cowering behind a parent, examining the contents of his pockets and from time to time glancing out at me mistrustfully.

The caller Otto had mentioned was waiting for me in the lobby of my hotel when I arrived there that evening, her slight frame bundled in a wet brown parka. A smirk crinkled her face as she caught my look of dismayed recognition. Margarete Menzer.

'There you are. Good. I heard about your father. Condolences. Do you have time for a drink?'

I couldn't think of an excuse, and lacked the bluntness to turn her down without one.

'All right,' I heard myself say.

We went into the hotel bar, a twilit place done up in sheet metal and rawhide, with a young crowd talking in loud voices over the pulsing beat of a synthetic drum.

'Chic hotel,' she said, grinning at a party of men with

194

shaved heads and elaborate underlip topiary. 'You must be selling lots of poems!'

'It's the cheapest place I could find.'

'You mean with gold taps and a private sauna!'

We found a dark nook and ordered drinks. She drank quickly: white wine, then vodka. Her hair, more frizzy now than curly, was tinged with grey; a mass of little iron springs. Her eyes, though, darting to and fro like a bird's above her sharp nose and chin, were black and shiny as ever. As they flickered over me, I felt the reassertion of the proprietorial interest she had taken in me from the start; the claim she had seemed to stake in me, as if recognising a member of her own species. 'It's good to see you again, Stefan,' she said, patting me lightly on the knee. 'I couldn't resist the chance of catching up when I found out you were coming over. I hope you don't mind?' I shook my head, wanting only to get this over with as quickly as possible. She had become a journalist, she told me, a freelancer for an Internet publication. 'Very cutting-edge,' she said with a grin, by which I took her to mean that she had found her way back into her old element of rumour and innuendo. She was single, she declared suddenly, with the overemphatic candour of someone who has consciously disinhibited herself. She took off her parka, revealing a surprisingly flimsy lace blouse. In it, the Margarete of my no doubt feverishly suspicious imagination was briefly supplanted by a possibly more objective Margarete: human, lonely, trying to look her best. A vodka or two later, she was asking if the bedrooms here were as funkily decorated as this bar. Was I tempted to offer to show her? Only out of a certain morbid curiosity; to find out what it would be like to occupy the blackest end of the spectrum of my possible selves. I resisted: 'No. They're very boring.' She chuckled. 'Still happily

195

married?' 'Extremely.' 'How nice.' Far from driving her off, my coldness seemed to cement her presence. She ordered more drinks, unpacked cigarettes from her purse and sank back into her seat with a contented look, as if we had just agreed to make a night of drinking and gossip.

'So,' she said, 'have you been back?'

'Back where?'

'Prenzlauer Berg, of course.'

'No.'

'You wouldn't recognise it. All chichi boutiques now.' She laughed, then gave a large, somewhat theatrical sigh: 'What a time that was! Those poets! All those crazy friends of my brother's, busy informing on each other day and night. No wonder they had a problem with plain language!' She glanced at me. 'You knew about that, right, the informing?' 'More or less.' 'My brother got most of the notoriety but they were all at it – Paul Boeden, Uwe Wardezky; Reinhard Kolbe's father was the Firm's own officer for cultural affairs!' I listened impassively as she continued, my face a mask of neutral attentiveness. She knocked back her drink – something staged in the recklessness of the gesture, I remember thinking, as though she felt it necessary to go through the motions of relinquishing self-control, for appearances' sake, before she could allow herself to unleash whatever mischief she had in mind. 'And it wasn't just the poets either,' she continued. 'Half the peace activists too. Sitting around discussing plans for some illegal anti-nuclear protest one minute, then scurrying off to tell their controls all about it! Hilarious, really! And nobody was above it. That's my considered opinion. Nobody at all. Not me, not you, not anyone. Amazing what a little fear will do to people!' She paused, drawing deeply on a cigarette and looking at me with a provocative grin, as if waiting for me to raise an objection. I was aware of a tightening in my chest, but I said nothing, not wanting to make things easier for her. 'The theatre people also,' she went on, blowing out her smoke, 'none of them had their hands clean. Not a single person. Not one.' She was locked on her target now, I could feel that; coursing forward on some riptide of malice. 'Benno Mautner,' she continued, 'he's the one who got the Stasi along for that swords-to-ploughshares performance —'

'All right Margarete —' I interrupted her.

'What? You don't remember? Where his actors all wore those insignias . . .'

'I remember, but —'

'But what? You don't want to hear?'

'Not really. I'm not that interested any more.'

'Well, here's something that'll interest you —'

It occurs to me that if I had allowed her to seduce me she might have spared me this. A purely chivalrous infidelity, that would have been! Protect the honour of your beloved by going to bed with her rival . . . But on the other hand, given her and her brother's peculiar gifts, she would more likely have found a way of having her cake and eating it.

'I doubt it,' I said.

'Inge.'

'Very funny.'

'Yes. Your lovely wife. Not then, but later.' Her eyes had darted up to gauge my reaction. 'You didn't know, did you? What I thought. Well, don't go blaming her. She had every right to turn on Thilo after he dumped her like that. Still, I heard that without her testimony they wouldn't have got the conviction that put him away. Your own contribution was apparently ruled inadmissible on account of your vested interest in the matter. You remember what sticklers for procedural correctness they were. Might as well have kept your hands clean! Wait – where are you going, Stefan? Have I upset you?'

I had stood up, and was putting on my coat.

'Don't be upset! No one cares about this shit any more –'

'Go to hell, Margarete,' I said, turning my back on her.

My body was trembling. I strode back across the lobby and on out through the revolving doors to the street. There was no question of my believing Margarete's repulsive slander, but just hearing it spoken, hearing Inge's name dragged like a shot-down swan through the mire of this goblinous procuress's vindictive imagination, was unbearable. If I could have foreseen that her brother was going to blackmail me a few years later, on precisely the basis of Inge's untarnished integrity, her absolute dissimilarity from myself and all these other fiends, I would have flung that in her face too (though, come to think of it, maybe my visceral reaction to Margarete's lies was in fact what gave Menzer the idea that I might be susceptible to blackmail in the first place!). I felt nauseous, dizzy, disgusted. Plunging blindly up past the Gendarmenmarkt, I found myself heading east on what must have been Karl-Liebknecht-Strasse, then before I knew it, crossing Alexanderplatz to Prenzlauer Allee. Only here did any thought of revisiting the old neighbourhood come to mind, and even then it was more a kind of helpless, passive gravitation than anything considered. The rain had thinned to a wet mist in which the new illuminations of the quarter shone glassily. Here were Saarbrücker Strasse, Metzer Strasse, Strassburger Strasse – so familiar and yet all so changed, as though I had travelled back in time only to find the past itself altered. The old brick warehouse with its barred portholes was gone, in its place a French *parfumerie*, the display cabinets behind its plate-glass window shedding a violet glow. I stared in, trying to picture the interior as it had been: an effort at first, as though the image were ashamed of its plainness in the face of the luxurious resplendence that had usurped it, and reluctant to be exhumed. But after a while I found myself imagining again the dark, tatty auditorium that had once occupied this space, and from there I was able to summon the figure of Inge as I had first beheld her, bringing her to mind in all her savage purity, until I could feel her luminous, incandescent spirit flooding into me once again, unblemished, purging the corrosive poison of Margarete's words, and shining inside me with the light of an inextinguishable reprieve. I can say in all truth that it has been burning there steadily ever since: my own figure of Liberty, standing sentinel at the threshold of my own incorruptible America.